EVERYTHING YOU WANT TO KNOW ABOUT FLYING—BUT WERE TOO SMART TO ASK

- How meals are cooked to perfection, using a simple formula: Blast at 275° for 35 minutes; to test, insert index finger and lick
- Flight Attendants' three job requirements: (1) Smile and say "Thank you" when someone hands you garbage; (2) Gracefully give a dinner party for 400 people in an hour and a half; (3) In case of a blazing inferno or other emergency, open the door, step aside and say, "After you!"
- Careful crew planning of layovers: Long Layover= 10 hours in Dayton; Short Layover= 36 hours in Paris
- Benefits of international travel: Time will seem to stand still (you won't know today's date), and you'll feel totally carefree (you won't remember your name)
- UFO sightings: No one in the cockpit will report the darting silver object hovering ahead, emitting blue lightning, because pilots prefer flying to selling used cars

PLUS Flight Attendant Training School's infamous hula-hoop test, how to be suspended from flying in Ten Easy Lessons, why the man sleeping next to you may be a well-disguised corpse...and more than you bargained for!

CABIN PRESSURE

**Elizabeth Harwell
and Corylee Spiro**

Illustrations by
HARRY TRUMBORE

ST. MARTIN'S PAPERBACKS

CABIN PRESSURE

Copyright © 1989 by Elizabeth Harwell and Corylee Spiro.

Illustrations by Harry Trumbore.

Library of Congress Catalog Card Number 89-4175

ISBN: 0-312-92121-7

Printed in the United States of America

St. Martin's Press hardcover edition published 1989
St. Martin's Paperbacks edition/July 1990

10 9 8 7 6 5 4 3 2 1

We'd like to dedicate this book to
Coral, Bill, Evelyn, Donald, Orville, and Wilbur

Contents

Acknowledgments

There would be no *Cabin Pressure* were it not for our dear co-workers, who daily cope with the rigors of flying through creative and, oftimes, irreverent behaviors. We cherish the comraderie that always seems to make even stressful situations endurable.

We'd like to thank our editor, Tom Dunne, for boldly allowing us to go where no flight attendants have gone before; David Hirshfeld, for maintaining his sanity when production deadlines often found all three of us thousands of miles apart; Matt Bialer, who always laughed at our stories while managing ten other tasks at the same time; our all-time favorite pilot, Captain Gil Lesko, who passed the pilot I.Q. test and also verified the accuracy of the more technical flight material; Biff Liff, whose kind and gentle manner always reassured us; and Barrie, wherever he may be, for invaluable introductions.

And, more than anyone, our agent, Michael Carlisle, for enthusiastic support, encouragement, and unending patience. Like Dorothy's Scarecrow, he gets the last and longest hug of all.

Introduction

We sat around the apartment one night laughing over all the things that happen in the airline industry. By the time we were rolling on the floor with hiccups, we realized we were on to something.

Since the onset of deregulation, more and different types of people have been traveling, airline companies have been expanding (also known as "merging"), and we have had one laugh after another. Just when we, as flight attendants, think we have seen it all, someone always provides us with something new in inflight entertainment.

Being confined with three hundred others in a small tube that's zooming around at 35,000 feet has a strange effect on the way "normal" people think and act. It's getting "caught in the act" that makes us roar.

Our intent has not been to point fingers at specific airlines (all names have been disguised to protect the guilty), but to make light of an industry that too often, we feel, is portrayed as the bad guy. Yes, the birds are stuffed to the gills, what you just ate *did* look like a hockey puck, and your scheduled arrival may be a tad delayed (two days). But if you knew the enormous number of variables that pertain to any flight, you'd marvel that the industry works AT ALL.

For the past year we have been collecting stories from other flight attendants, pilots, agents, mechanics—anyone connected with the industry. Having worked in commercial aviation for a combined total of eighteen years, we can accept that, to the best of insiders' knowledge, these anecdotes are TRUE. We simply ask you to keep this in mind as you're shaking your head in disbelief.

It has been our experience that no matter where we are people love to hear the funny stories. We've laughed, and now we feel it's time to share these outrageous antics of the air with you.

Fasten your seatbelts, relax, and PREPARE FOR DEPARTURE!!

PART
I

GETTING
ACQUAINTED

CANCELED YOU'VE GOT TO BE KIDDING MY BAGS BETTER
BE ON THIS FLIGHT PLEASE LET ME USE THE FIRST CLASS
LAV IT'S EMPTY AND I'M GOING TO EMBARRASS MYSELF
LOOK I *WAS* HERE AN HOUR IN ADVANCE AND I DON'T
SMOKE I SMOKE AND I CAN'T SIT FIVE HOURS WITHOUT
ONE YOU'RE TAKING BOTH ARMRESTS AND DROOLING
MOVE OVER WOULD YOU PLEASE JUST SHUUUT UUUP MY
GOD I CAN'T SIT NEXT TO THAT SCREAMING BABY FOR
SEVEN HOURS I WANTED THE CHICKEN IT IS CHICKEN OH
SHIT STAIRS TO THE GROUND WHAT IF I HAD BEEN
CHOKING TO DEATH IN THIS SEAT WOULD YOU COME
THEN I DEMAND TO SEE THE HEAD FLIGHT ATTENDANT I
NEED A DRINK NOW PLEASE GOD DON'T LET THEM GIVE
HIM ANOTHER DRINK *THAT'S* NOT MY LUGGAGE IS IT I
DON'T DESERVE THIS TREATMENT I AM A FREQUENT
FLYER DAMN IT NO PROBLEM WITH THE LANDING GEAR
CAN BE SLIGHT THEY'RE GOING TO HEAR ABOUT THIS!

Thank you so much DEREGULATION! What has happened
to the world of aviation? . . . To those beautiful astrojets
with the comfort of your living room? . . . To on-time
departures? . . . To the glamour girls of the skies? . . .
Where did it all go?

Well, folks, the days of Coffee, Tea, or Me are gone. The
astrojets of the sixties have turned into the flying sardine
cans of the eighties, and on-time departures are now defined
as those leaving within twenty-four hours of schedule.

On the bright side, deregulation has worked to the

benefit of each of you. No longer do Dorothy and Toto need the Good Witch of the North to get them back to Kansas: We can get them there for a mere $99 (with five stopovers—significant restrictions apply).

Yes, of course we love it; we're enraptured with flying; aviation is our *life!* This poem, written in 1941, is as meaningful today as it was then.

HIGH FLIGHT

Oh, I have slipped the surly bonds of earth[1]
   And danced the skies on laughter-silvered wings;[2]
Sunward I've climbed,[3] and joined the tumbling
     mirth[4]
Of sun-split clouds[5]—and done a hundred things
You have not dreamed of [6]—wheeled and soared and
     swung[7]
   High in the sunlit silence.[8] Hov'ring there,[9]
I've chased the shouting wind along,[10] and flung
   My eager craft through footless halls of air.[11]
Up, up the long, delirious, burning blue[12]
   I've topped the windswept heights[13] with easy grace
Where never lark, or even eagle flew.[14]
   And, while with silent, lifting mind I've trod
The high untrespassed sanctity of space,[15]
   Put out my hand, and touched the face of God.[16]

                —John Gillespie Magee, Jr.

Federal Aviation Administration Supplement

1. Flight crews must insure that all surly bonds have been slipped entirely before interacting with the traveling public, as any detectable trace of an onboard surly bond slip may be grounds for termination.

2. During periods of severe sky dancing, the Fasten Seatbelt sign must remain continuously illuminated.

3. Use of Ace bandage–type support hose and similarly confining undergarments is strongly recommended for those who climb sunward often.

4. Joining the tumbling mirth is prohibited to pilots and flight attendants on duty if the mirth is taking place in the lavatory, as joining this action wholly constitutes "conduct unbecoming a flight crewmember."

5. Pilots must not exceed 30 degrees of bank while flying in clouds forecast to be sun-split, as doing so will result in flight-attendant uniform splits as well.

6. Do not perform these hundred things in front of (a) Federal Aviation Administration inspectors, (b) flight supervisors, or (c) frequent flyers.

7. Wheeling, soaring, and swinging will not be accomplished simultaneously except by pilots in the flight simulator on their own time.

8. Be advised that *sunlit* silence will occur only while transporting an entire flight of deaf-mutes.

9. "Hov'ring there" will constitute a highly reliable signal that a flight emergency is imminent.

10. Flight-attendant regulations state that although chasing of the Shouting Wind is allowed, chasing of the shouting children is *not*.

11. Be forewarned that pilot craft-flinging is a leading cause of flight attendant/passenger injury.

12. Should any crewmember or passenger experience delirium while in the burning blue, submit an irregularity report upon flight termination.

13. Windswept heights will be topped by a minimum of 1,000 feet to prevent massive airsickness-bag use.

14. When larks or eagles *are* flying, flight attendants are encouraged to upgrade the inflight meal service to include an additional (fowl) entrée choice by procuring resultant engine-ingested remnants.

15. Air Traffic Control (ATC) must issue all special releases for trodding the high untrespassed sanctity of space.

16. Federal Aviation Administration regulations state that *no one* may sacrifice aircraft cabin pressure to open windows/doors in order to touch God's face.

As you can imagine, an airline is a major operation—even more complex than the United States postal system (you don't have to feed the mail). It takes the combined efforts of hundreds of people to bungle a job this big.

It's time to introduce the players.

Your initial contact will most likely be made with "reservations"—some preconceived ones that you will have, and a separate airline department that will provide others for you. You will speak over the telephone with either a saint (if you place your call during the weekdays—this is their primary source of supplemental income) or, alternately, a robot (saints are busy on weekends). They will always treat you with the utmost respect and patience, because they are being neither stepped or vomited on nor screamed at. Cherish and celebrate them while you can.

The "ticket agents" will be first on your agenda once you reach the airport. These people will also show you great kindness provided you do not piss them off. Their job description imbues them with major, secret decision-making capabilities regarding the ultimate destination of your luggage. You have a mouth that you can use to rectify any mistakes in your routing—your luggage does *not*.

Your next careful (if you're smart) step will be with the gate agent. This person has truly awesome powers over your more immediate happiness. During peak travel times, the situation may begin to disintegrate rapidly at this point. If you wish to sit on the plane next to the three-year-old child traveling with you, be nice.

You ought to be excited now. It's nearly time to get on board and meet your flight crew—the peacocks of the industry. Bring gifts: Candy and flowers are always appropriate.

The "flight attendants" are the onboard police officers who also double as waitresses, and the "pilots" are the people who have the best seats up front and make the houses on the ground get smaller or larger. Both groups talk funny: "Did you pull up your bids yet? I was bid denied and then put on availability, and month after next is my reserve rotation. I brought in circle time, so I'm illegal for my first outbound—it's an 8 in 24 or a 30 in 7 problem. Listen, did we ever receive that understaffing and gate-holding pay for the turnaround on the 26th? I wasn't aware that . . ."

On board, they say things like, "Would you care for a predeparture beverage?" which means, "Do you want a drink before we go?" It's all very confusing.

Let's not forget those "behind-the-scenes" people that are important, too: the maintenance men, baggage handlers, ground crews, caterers, cabin-service personnel, air traffic and ramp controllers, and so on. All of these individuals have the opportunity to make your trip memorable—one way or another.

Then there are the "suck-and-blow" machines themselves: widebody airplanes—747's, DC10's, L1011's, 767's, A-300's, and so forth—whose gross weight on take-off exceeds 300,000 pounds (you would have been happier all your life not knowing *that,* right?), and narrow-body airplanes—727's, 737's, 757's, DC9's, et cetera—which have only one aisle down the middle and never show movies. For one reason or another, we each have our favorite airplanes to work on, and we bid trips accordingly.

In days gone by, airlines showed real originality in their interior decor. Years ago, when the entire flight experience from start to finish was a peaceful and serene one, the cabin interior looked like this:

Now, it looks like this:

It has a calming effect (you'll be thankful for that), and graffiti and chewing gum removal is much easier.

The arrival and departure facilities for our silver chariots are pretty amazing themselves. When you consider that these mega-airports, with 7 runways, 40 miles of taxiways, 50 million square feet of concrete, football fields of parking space, 15 terminals, restaurants, bookstores, boutiques, popcorn stands, video arcades, shoe-repair booths, car-rental stalls, moving sidewalks, elevators, and escalators, have all evolved from that ancient and primitive Peruvian landing strip of the "gods" (which didn't even have a toilet), you oughta be impressed.

Barbie Dolls,
Golden Girls,
and Fairy Tales

When we were first hired, we had no idea what the job really entailed. We were all lured in by visions of a glamorous life and the opportunity to travel and interact with different cultures (most of which have turned out to be bacterial). Our training was a far cry from reality. It certainly didn't prepare us mentally for the full impact of what we had agreed IN WRITING to perform for a large corporation.

Speaking from first-hand experience, we know we must be crazy. You do, too—just think about it for a moment.

What sane person would be remotely interested in a job that required him or her to:

1. Smile and say "thank you" when someone handed over garbage,

2. Gracefully give a dinner party for four hundred people in an hour and a half, and

3. In the case of a blazing inferno or other emergency, open the door, step aside and say, "AFTER YOU!"?

As a newly hired flight attendant, you're like a pledge rushing a sorority. You'll be taken to task daily by your co-workers, so you'll want to be on your toes. Learning to get along with your crewmembers is your first and most important step. Here's a glimpse at some of the people you are going to be working with.

THE GOLDEN GIRLS.   Other airlines may refer to them as "crinklies," "dinosaurs," or "jetbags." Do not ask them if they knew the Wright brothers.

THE DITSIES.   Somehow managing survival with an I.Q. lower than their age, they walk through the aisles with a glazed look. If you have a problem with irate passengers, send these people to the rescue. They'll have the passengers so confused that they'll forget whatever it was they were angry about. Do not worry about making them mad— they're incapable of recognizing an insult.

THE FAIRY TAILS.   When the rest of the world is on 33 these boys are spinning around at 78. For the most part they possess a delightfully irreverent outlook on life and will have you howling in the aisles. Do not make jokes about an "AC/DC10."

THE OSCAR NOMINEES. Give them an audience and watch them perform. Do not *dare* to upstage them.

Why do you need to know these things? How can we tell if you're new, anyway? Because, you're easy to spot. You're the one:

1. Who will aid in a passenger's decision to commit himself as he's frantically searching for his return-trip ticket (on the flight out yesterday; you took it, too)

2. Who, after spilling coffee in a passenger's crotch, will attempt to mop it up

3. Who, on the autobahn en route to the hotel, will ask "Well, where *is* Ausfart?"

Chances are this poor flight attendant (on opposite page) is on "reserve." Each month the company requires a certain number of flight attendants to sit on call. This back-up system ensures crew manning on greatly delayed flights whose crews have gone "illegal," upline cancellations that require a "flight origination" to occur in a downline city, and those flights that are missing a flight attendant because he/she had the audacity to get sick.

The reserve system is a contractual arrangement whose setup varies from carrier to carrier. At some airlines, you'll be on reserve until you are senior enough (relative to flight attendants employed after you were) to hold a regularly scheduled trip. At other airlines, you'll be on reserve on a

NOTES ON "RESERVE"

(Review these when you feel you're losing your grip)

Passengers, have you ever gotten on an airplane expecting to see this . . .

But seen this, instead?

rotating basis—perhaps one month on, one month off—regardless of seniority. That's basically the arrangement we're familiar with (with myriad variations that would make for very dull reading here).

In essence, the company owns our souls during these periods, and it's their chance to get even. Your brother is getting married? You have a black-tie affair to go to? So what? You're going somewhere on a three-day trip. (Tough luck.) In our eyes, it's one very long night of the living dead. Here's the progression of what happens to the body and mind of a flight attendant on call.

WEEK ONE: Every time the phone rings, your heart shuts down temporarily, causing your blood pressure to plummet and your respiration to drop to zombie level. Your stomach tenses from stress, and you start popping Di-Gel. Most flight attendants learn this the hard way, but DO NOT ANSWER THE PHONE EVEN ON YOUR DAYS OFF. Once crew schedule gets you, they have you. Have your roommate tell them you're in the shower. (If they call back in five hours, you're *still* in the shower.) Do not talk to them because, if you do, you can't say no; you have to go!

WEEK TWO: Due to the fact that you were not available to fly on your days off, you have progressed to the top of their SHIT LIST (now you will know why the term *screw schedule* came into being). There will be no way to salvage the remainder of the month. During this week you will fly an "all-nighter" followed by a 5 A.M. sign-in. Of course, this kind of circadian flip-flop is wonderful for your health. Your face will look like a cheese pizza by the end of the week. (DON'T SQUEEZE.)

WEEK THREE: You're on the very brink of insanity at this point. Uncontrollable twitching starts as the phone rings at 2 A.M. You are ordered to go back to sleep for now, but to be at the airport by 6 A.M. You stare at the ceiling for two hours, and as you drift into a peaceful sleep . . . IT'S TIME TO WAKE UP!!

WEEK FOUR: With dark circles under your sunken eyeballs, and sitting with a sledgehammer across your lap, you eagerly wait by the phone, slobbering all over yourself. Your uniform is filthy, and your hair looks like a grass mat. The thing rings. You pulverize it.

The thirtieth of the month comes, and you've made it in one piece. You have thirty days to recover and buy a new telephone, so that you can do this again!

Being a tightly knit group, we look out for the new ones. After all, we were there once, too. Here are some helpful tips we've come up with to make their lives easier.

1. *Take care of your skin.* Because of the dryness of the airplane cabin, go to work looking like "I've been slimed" from the three inches of moisturizers you'll wear. It's like being inflight larvae: You go in all gooey in the beginning and come out all dried and mature at the other end.

2. *Learn the language.* There are four phrases that you will use repeatedly during every flight (the first three must be said all in one breath): "Excuse me," "Please," "I'm sorry," and "Chicken or beef?"

3. *Little white lies never hurt.* During "irregular operations," the ones you'll get the most mileage out of are: "I'm sure you'll make your connection," "Chances are, your bags will, too," "The company will put you up overnight if you don't make your connection," "We will be leaving shortly," and "I'll be right back."

4. *Leave your habits at the "office."* When you're out on a date, make sure that you SIT DOWN before you start to eat your meal. Leave the tablecloth and your date's jacket alone. Use the white, folded object sitting at the left of your plate to wipe your mouth and/or nose.

You're well on your way to fitting in. After a while the job will be second nature. You'll be taking those corners with your wheelies faster than Andy Granatelli, and you will figure out how to get your 34-inch hips down that 12-inch-wide aisle without a single bruise.

There's one final exam that must be taken before you complete your six-month probationary period. Let's see how much you've learned from your "on-the-job" training.

THE FINAL EXAM

As a flight attendant, you will be faced with many situations that require quick decisions. Consider each question carefully and choose the solution that is most in line with your co-workers' way of thinking. (The correct answer follows each question. No peeking.)

1. During the meal service you pull out a tray from your mobile aisle cart, and the roll falls to the floor. You

know that you are catered for the exact number of passengers on board. Do you:

A. Discard the roll, then apologize and explain to the passenger why he will not receive a roll, apologize and explain to the passenger why he will not receive a roll, apologize and explain to the passenger why HE WILL NOT RECEIVE A ROLL!!?

B. Smile enthusiastically, serve the roll, wink, and tell the dumbfounded passenger that he'll soon find out if cabin services' claim that "these airplanes are so clean, you could eat off the floor" is TRUE?

C. Switch that roll with one on another tray (passengers ten rows down won't suspect a thing)?

ANSWER: C

2. An irate passenger approaches you and asks for the name of one of your co-workers. She wants to complain to the company about the flight attendant's behavior. Do you:

A. Emphatically agree that the flight attendant is no good (explaining that management and the flight corps have wanted a reason to get rid of her for a long time) and suggest the passenger fill out a complaint form before the end of the flight that you *personally* guarantee will wind up in the right hands. UPON RECEIPT, TOSS IN GARBAGE CAN.

B. Cunningly arrange for an onboard face-off between the uninformed flight attendant in question and the passenger, assembling the crew to watch?

C. Write down the name of a flight attendant you can't *stand* and give it to the irate passenger. Wait for guilt to overcome you.

ANSWER: A

3. You have been forewarned by the agent that the passenger sitting in 5B has already had a lot to drink and asked to please limit the amount of liquor he consumes. Do you do so by:

A. Refusing to serve him another drink, thereby causing an onboard riot?

B. Telling him that orange juice is much better for his health?

C. Keeping track of how many swizzle sticks are accumulating on his tray table and, when the number reaches four, cutting him off by handing him liquor "minis" containing appropriately colored soft drinks?

ANSWER: C

4. You have been circling Chicago for one hour because of bad weather conditions. You are aware that most of the passengers have connecting flights. Do you:

A. Go into the aisles with the Official Airline Guide and a hand-held computer to help reroute them to their final destinations?

B. Announce that they will all make their flights because the airline has decided to hold all departures until they have landed?

C. Hide in the galley?

ANSWER: B or C

5. You are on a five-hour flight. Toward the end of the meal service you realize you are fourteen meals short. Do you:

A. Tell the passengers that there will be meal vouchers waiting for them once they land?

B. Offer complimentary alcoholic beverages to numb their hunger pangs?

C. Have a flight attendant retrieve uneaten food portions from the forward part of the cabin and reconstruct from this garbage a close approximation of a "virgin meal"?

ANSWER: B (This is a trick question. At first glance answer C seems the logical choice. However, C may provoke noticeable side effects, for instance, death, ultimately causing you much more trouble than it was worth.)

Get your hands out of the post office box! No matter how much you now wish you had *never* mailed in your flight-attendant application, tampering with the United States mail is against the law. And a felony charge will do you no good in your pursuit of more respectable employment . . .

We accept your gratitude.

✈

Sometimes what people say to us surely isn't what they mean.

On one of our flights from San Diego to Chicago, several children on board believed that the red flight-attendant call button was a fun plaything because it made a little bell ring throughout the cabin. We answered those bells about thirty times and were apologized to by the respective parents each time we reached their seats.

An East Indian male passenger traveling with us was thirsty again after the initial beverage and meal service. He rang the service call button above his head (the square button depicting a skirted stewardess), but no one responded. He became disgruntled, assuming that the service was shoddy.

One stewardess had been doing a walk-through of the cabin when the annoyed man grabbed her, pointed to the call button, and said in broken English, "I have been fingering this stewardess for the past twenty minutes, and NO ONE'S COME YET!"

"Well, I'm sorry, sir," she sweetly replied. "The flight attendants on this flight are a little older, so it takes them longer to come."

✈

When an airplane is taxiing out, taking off, flying below 10,000 feet, landing, and taxiing in, the Federal Aviation Administration mandates a blackout in cockpit and cabin crew nonsafety-related communications. These periods are known as "sterile cockpit."

At the last minute, an agent on one flight threw the remaining thirty standby passengers onto the plane and closed the door, and the captain started to push back from the gate. The problem was that the plane now had seventeen more passengers on board than available seats.

The inexperienced head flight attendant went to the cockpit to relay the problem. As she opened the door, the indignant captain screamed at her, "We're sterile."

"Captain, I don't care what your sexual problems are, but we have seventeen people back here without seats."

Amuse Airlines had a charming way of ending each flight. The number one flight attendant would stand in the jetbridge on deplaning and hand individually wrapped mints to each passenger. As passengers were normally weighted down with carry-on luggage and would not have a free hand to receive them, it became a game as to where to plant the mint on the person. The flight attendant would always make light of the passengers' burdens by making some stupid quip.

"My, looks like you could use just one more hand there," she said to a loaded-down passenger as she stuck the mint in his shirt pocket. His smile changed to a very sad frown; and as he walked away, the flight attendant became heartsick as she noticed that he was a right-arm amputee.

One afternoon on a DC10 flight from LaGuardia to Dallas, Abby (a voluptuous redhead from Louisiana) took a few moments after the service to chat with the fellows in the cockpit. She had been on the line only about six months and was still in the learning stages.

Knowing the pay-scale progression of flight attendants, and being aware of the extra pay given for working the more demanding cabin positions, she asked how the pilots' pay structure worked. Was their pay strictly by seniority? Or did prior military qualifications, for instance, have any bearing?

"Well," the captain responded, "there are three separate pay scales for us as we upgrade from flight engineer to first officer and, finally, reach full captain status."

"So, basically, your three pay scales work on yearly 'per

hour' raises, and you reach maximum pay after twelve years like we do?" She was trying so hard to make sense of it all.

Wanting her to grasp the picture in its entirety, the captain continued. "That's right, but with one major difference. We're also paid strictly according to size of equipment."

"Well, that's disgusting!" she cried indignantly as she shook her head in disbelief. "I certainly hope your union is fighting it. God, how unfair!!"

Aircraft type, Abby. Aircraft type.

We had worked our New York/Los Angeles flight with a girl who, at least to Cory, didn't have all her oars in the water. Knowing we'd work the return trip together the next day, I felt guilty for not knowing her name.

"Cory," I said in my southern accent over dinner, "What was that girl's name? I never did find out." Looking at the girl sitting across the room, Cory said laughingly in Staten Islandese, "Oh, her? Ditsy. Ditsy's her name."

The next day's flight was not a pleasant one. I couldn't understand why, but I was being snubbed by at least two of my co-workers. On the bus on the way home, I cornered Cory.

"Cory, did you notice that Ditsy and her friend really don't like me?" Cory laughed. The southerner caught on fast. She'll be a New Yorker in no time.

"Well, no, I didn't notice. But it was a very busy flight. What did you do to them?"

"Nothing as far as I can tell."

"Well, when did it start?"

"About twenty minutes after take-off. I said, 'How was your layover, Ditsy?' and she just walked off."

"You said, 'Ditsy'?"

"Yes, that's her name, isn't it?"

"Oh, God, Liz. You dummy, Ditsy means dumbo, stupid . . . uh, spacy, you know—no dots on the dice!"

It took two weeks of apologies to convince the girl that that word was an unknown in my vocabulary. Oh well, at least I've taken the price tags off my hats.

✈

After our flight into Los Angeles International, the entire flight crew was waiting outside the terminal for the crew limo van to take us to our hotel. The usual recording, "The white zone is for loading and unloading; the blue zone . . ." stuff was playing continuously in the background.

One of the junior crewmembers was very upset and expressed her concern to the crew. "Can you imagine how boring that job would be? I mean, sitting there all day just saying that over and over again?"

And she was serious!

✈

It was a beautifully still, clear autumn day. During this early-morning flight the pilots had commented to each other how lovely the neighboring jet contrails were—straight, white streaks of jet steam across the deep blue sky. They joked about how they hoped they would never have to get a real job. Life was good.

After her meal service duties were finished, a young flight attendant decided to visit the cockpit for a few minutes of R and R. As she sat behind the captain in the elevated cockpit jumpseat, she had a bird's-eye view of the world.

"Fellows, look at that down on the ground." Perplexed, she was unknowingly setting herself up.

"I'm looking, Carol," the captain answered. "Don't see anything unusual. What are you pointing to, dear?"

"There's a thin, straight black line on the ground down there. Look how long it is!"

Realizing that the girl was seeing the thin but distinct shadow that their own contrail was casting on the earth below, the captain replied, "Oh, now I see it. Carol, you're very lucky to be up here right now. This is very rare, but I guess the light must be just right today. That happens to be the state line between Massachusetts and Vermont. It is Massachusetts and Vermont, isn't it, fellas?"

"Oh, yes, definitely between Massachusetts and Vermont," the guys answered, fighting to suppress their laughter.

As she left the cockpit shaking her head at the amazements of life, Carol said, "My God, I've been flying for three years and, can you believe, I never knew about that?"

Maybe you will have the luck of the Irish and get on a flight on which the president of the airline is traveling. During a previous brain-jarring landing, we had blown two tires. Normal time to change a tire is about one hour, but someone must have fed the mechanics speed, or threatened them with death, because somehow they managed to change those tires in fifteen minutes flat.

A brand-new flight attendant approached Mr. Ladnarc after take-off, and in a very sweet and innocent voice said, "Mr. Ladnarc, I would love to fly with you all the time—this is how we were told in training our trips would be. But in the past six months this is the first time we've been catered properly, left on time, or had a problem fixed so fast."

Out of the mouths of babes!

Upon boarding, a male passenger noticed a female flight attendant crawling on all fours between two rows of seats. Wanting to be helpful, he said, "Miss, are you looking for something?"

Tired and food stained, she replied, "Yes, sir. I guess I'm looking for all that glamour they promised me in training."

It was a 95-degree summer evening, and the air conditioning on the aircraft was not up to snuff. The thought of putting on our knee-length, polyester, front-closure, wrap-around serving toppers over our wool gabardine uniforms made all of us sweat. Being the practical one among us, Suzanne decided that her skirt and pantyhose were coming off; no one would be the wiser, and she'd be comfortable.

After finishing an uneventful meal service in the cabin, she went to serve the cockpit their meals. Standing in front of the cockpit door with one meal tray in hand, she started to reach for her cockpit keys, which she always kept in her uniform skirt pocket. Forgetting that she had taken off her skirt, she pulled her serving topper widely apart preparing to dig into one of her nonexistent side pockets.

The entire first class got some very private inflight entertainment, Suzanne's special "Moonlight Serenade."

Ned O'Toole is a very lazy male flight attendant. As we walked down the aisle of the airplane, a passenger requested a beverage from him.

"Oh, I'm the pilot, ma'am. Why don't you just ask one

of the girls for a drink. I'm sure they'll be more than happy to help you."

We could have killed him!

✈

The van carrying the entire crew was driving back to New York after an unscheduled landing in a city our carrier didn't normally serve. As it drove past Brielle, New Jersey's Yacht Club, one flight attendant known more for her capacity for empathy than for intelligence remarked, "Oh, you guys look. That is so nice. A special yacht club just for the blind."

✈

Debbie, the head flight attendant, was so busy setting up on board for a flight that she didn't get a chance to get the enroute information from the pilot. Beth, her flying partner, offered to obtain it for her and almost fell over when she entered the cockpit.

A pilot named Captain Fhung sat poised for action on two fat pillows. He had on black leather gloves and looked like he was ready to race a Yamaha.

Coming out of the cockpit, Beth mischievously decided to change the flight information a tad. At pushback, she handed the slightly altered data sheet to Debbie, who picked up the microphone and began the routine announcements:

"Good morning, ladies and gentlemen. We'd like to welcome you on board Allegiance Airlines' Flight 59 to San Francisco." Debbie glanced down to verify the flight number and the captain's name from the data sheet before continuing. "In command of our aircraft today is Captain DUNG and . . ." Before she could finish, laughter bellowed throughout the cabin. Beth, the culprit, made a swift exit.

Captain "Dung" became a popular pilot as passengers stopped by the cockpit before deplaning to check out the little shit . . .

✈

It was a very hectic flight, and the head flight attendant grabbed one of the new flight attendants working the trip. "Would you please go up front and help pick up first-class trays?" she asked.

Unable to recall what she knew must be a special procedure for doing this, the new flight attendant asked, "How do I pick up a first-class tray?"

"The way you've been picking up all the male passengers this month—fast!" the head flight attendant replied.

✈

The five-member cabin crew included one who was obviously a different variety: She wore huge, red rhinestone earrings and had short, blue-streaked, spiked hair. Seeming to notice this fact, a rather conservative male passenger made a point of asking where we were all based.

"Well, the four of us are from Chicago, but she's L.A.-based."

Shaking his head in disbelief, he replied, "No, dear. She's free-based."

✈

A "ditsy" flight attendant was desperately trying to make conversation with a good-looking first-class passenger.

Groping for something to talk about, she noticed they had similar tie bars. She pointed to his and said, "Oh, we've got something in common, only you've got balls and I've got boxes."

A female passenger was talking to an older flight attendant during a flight. "You've been flying for such a long time. Aren't you afraid of never having a husband?"

The flight attendant looked at her sweetly, winked, and said, "Oh, don't worry about me. I've had *many* husbands."

✈

A senior flight attendant went up to the cockpit to introduce herself. As she opened the door, she was shocked to see three very young pilots sitting there.

Incredulous, she exclaimed, "Oh my God, I have clothes hanging in my closet that are older than the three of you!"

✈

Peter, Larry, and Tom decided to jet over to France for a ski weekend. Peter reassured the others that he had a full command of French and to leave everything to him.

Once settled in the chalet, it was off to the slopes. As they rode up the lift, Larry asked Peter what each sign meant, and Peter was happy to oblige. "See that sign. That's the important one. It means 'this way down.'"

Midway down the slopes, Larry and Tom realized that Peter wasn't as fluent as they thought. The sign actually meant 'rocks.'

The three survived the trip to the bottom with only a few bruises, put in a full day of skiing, and by nightfall were more than ready for a nice, relaxing evening. Entering the chalet, Peter looked at a sign and announced, "Okay guys, this is just what the doctor ordered—a sauna." They dropped their equipment in their rooms, took off their clothes, and went to the sauna in towels and slippers. To their great embarrassment, they opened the door and found themselves in the middle of . . . a nightclub!

Peter has yet to live it down.

Joe and Sonja were working on the liquor cart and both noticed a very attractive, distinguished man sitting in an aisle seat. As they approached his row, Joe turned to the man and complimented him.

"Nice head of hair," he said, immediately catching the daggars being thrown his way by the person sitting next to him who was completely bald.

Open mouth, insert both feet.

Cocks
in the
Pit

Although no one has figured out the exact origin of the term *cockpit* (flight attendants as a group make no claim to be linguists), our experiences on the job have clarified this obscure terminology for us. Yes, it's true that the people in command of these commercial jet aircraft are highly trained professionals. Most of them are polite, courteous individuals whose calm exteriors are excited by nothing short of a blazing bonfire beneath their butts. But they're not without their idiosyncrasies.

Pilots themselves define their jobs as "great periods of

boredom punctuated by moments of sheer terror." After take-off recently, we entered the cockpit to bring up the usual container of soft drinks and coffee. We were barely acknowledged by three men thoroughly engrossed in their morning newspapers.

"How's it going, captain?" Cory offered as a friendly greeting. Glancing up at us over his bifocals, he replied in monotone, "It's terrifying."

The one thing most flight attendants *will* tell you is that pilots are cheap, cheap, cheap. Perhaps it's because so many of them have multiple families to support, or maybe it's just a common personality quirk. We know of one captain who made the *Guiness Book of Records* because he actually *purchased* a newspaper. Mostly, they just scavenge the paper-strewn cabin after the first flight of the day, before the cabin cleaners come on to collect the garbage. (And if they thought the company would let them pocket refunds for nonused layover hotel rooms, they'd certainly be traveling with sleeping bags.)

The layover attire of almost all pilots consists of a golf shirt with some kind of animal logo on the left breast and those polyester pants with the two-inch waistbands. Their penchant for synthetic fiber britches along with the afore-mentioned breeding tendencies has caused us to affection-ately nickname them collectively the Double-Knit-Wit-Pit.

If this sounds like sour grapes, it's all in good fun. Flight attendants go out of their way to make these stoic daredevils comfortable. We've hoarded so many packages of honey-roasted airline peanuts for them that the Golden Eagle Company has considered renaming the product Pilot Pel-lets. Besides, the pilots have lots of chances to get even.

After a while we tend to distrust everything we see and hear in the cockpit (this is probably to our *great* benefit).

Kathleen was in the cockpit one night when a pilot invited her to view Mars through a tiny side window–mounted telescope. She'd been enraptured for about five minutes when he told her that the faint red planet she was seeing was a work light glowing at its lowest reostat setting. Ha. Ha. Ha.

Once on a DC9, the first officer called back and directed us to send the captain back up to the cockpit immediately. Not being aware that he'd left, we canvassed the cabin in search of the man. All toilets were vacant, and he was nowhere to be found. We entered the cockpit to relay the distressing news and must have looked pretty upset because the first officer decided to end the little joke. He pushed the captain's seat all the way forward and knocked on a panel that had previously been under the chair. The captain sheepishly crawled out of the nose gear wheel well. Thanks, fellas.

Pilots are great jokers all right. We've seen them pull a DC10 up to the gate at JFK and scare the agent to death because they were all wearing three-foot-long dreadlock wigs—a sight that had to be seen to be believed. And we know one guy who exited the cockpit after his last (very last) flight on October 31, dressed like a Wookie. He was mumbling something about hyperspace as the gate agent meeting the flight dialed the chief pilot to complain about the incident.

And then there was one captain's PA announcement that managed to elevate everyone's heart rate, at least temporarily: "Uh, we're number one for departure. Would the flight attendants prepare for take-off . . . And ladies and gentlemen, please check to be sure your seatbelts are securely fastened—we're going to try something." Gird your loins.

One of their favorite and most effective ploys is to begin an unannounced take-off roll after a thirty-minute taxi-out hold, when all the flight attendants are gossiping over coffee in the mid-galley. We guess it is pretty funny to see twelve of us scurrying like roaches under fire to our respective jumpseats at the far corners of a DC10. Of course, the cockpit crew is always *sooo* sorry they forgot to cue us over the PA with "Flight attendants, please prepare for departure."

Captains have truly great opportunities to get us during taxiing. We've seen flight attendants literally disappear between passenger rows during safety demos, courtesy of the overzealous driving habits of these fun-loving gentlemen. (And ladies, please note: When the cockpit comprises two or more female pilots during any given inflight segment, said cockpit shall henceforth be referred to as the Box Office.)

And let's not forget how effective it is to fly a widebody jet with its nose cruising twenty feet higher than its tail. Pushing 250-pound beverage carts around on that kind of incline makes those pretty, purple veins in our legs pop right out.

But, that's okay. Fair's fair. They certainly are good sports. The other day one pilot asked us, "What separates flight attendants from the lowest life form known to man?" Before we could defend ourselves, he answered, "The cockpit door."

Yes, they've made quite a reputation for themselves. The expression, "Positive climb, gear up, rings off!" is not for naught. I have seen a couple of wedding rings suspiciously disappear as soon as those main gear wheels leave the runway.

Their favorite saying of late is "telephone, telegraph, tell-a-flight attendant." Yes, we are enthusiastic gossips! But that's hardly surprising when we overhear comments from them like, "Too bad our trip's over. Now it's time to leave our loved ones and go home."

We should be more forgiving. Maybe it's just that they have a problem with using language correctly. Remember, these are people who have been trained to casually state that "We have a *slight* problem with the landing gear." Now we all know in our hearts that there is no such thing as a "slight" problem with the landing gear.

We've included the following restricted information to help you appreciate more fully the enormous mental capacity of these brave, courageous, stout-hearted, impudent, brazen, crazed individuals. So it's not *Top Gun*. Only a few (thousand) will make it through this particularly grueling final test, allowing them to at least join the ranks of the "Best of the Rest."

PILOT I.Q. TEST

1. Which is larger?

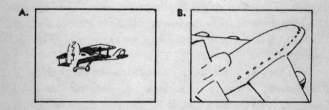

A.

B.

2. Which would you be more likely to mate with effectively?

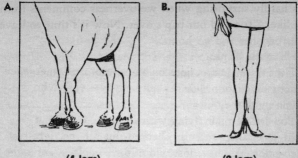

A.

(4 legs)

B.

(2 legs)

3. (This question tests facility in interpreting complex computer graphic data.)
   In which figure do the two lines apparently merge?

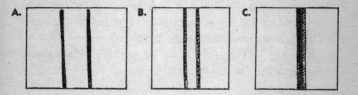

A. **B.** **C.**

4. How many families can you reasonably support after ten years of service with your airline?

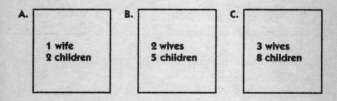

A.
1 wife
2 children

B.
2 wives
5 children

C.
3 wives
8 children

5. *Flight* is to *crash*, as *layover* is to:
   A. stewardess
   B. paradise
   C. free hors d'oeuvres
   D. alimony

6. Fill in the blank:
   The printed instructions on a nonautomatic emergency door evacuation slide say JERK TO INFLATE. Who do you think they mean? _____.

7. You are a captain flying with a newly hired flight engineer and a recently checked-out-for-the-right-seat co-pilot. You have lost two of three engines, are in the middle of a massive hail storm, and are not sure your landing gear is down and locked. Choose the appropriate color for your uniform trousers:
   A. Navy blue   B. Gray   C. Dark greenish-brown

8. An important judgment call must be made. Your initial conclusion is that 2 + 2 = 3. After additional research is done by the rest of the cockpit crew and all pertinent facts are in, your final analysis is that 2 + 2 =
   A. 3   B. 3   C. 3   D. All of the above.

9. Choose the dissimilar item:

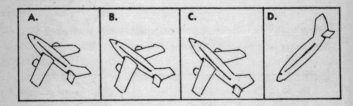

10. The most useless thing on a flight attendant is:
    A. False eyelashes
    B. Fake nails
    C. Fifty-year-old captains

Okay, okay . . . maybe we should give them a break. Perhaps their brains are fried from the hours of stress spent in the flight "stimulator." You decide. The stories that follow speak for themselves . . .

✈

A captain was known systemwide for his unwelcome sexual advances on layovers. One flight attendant he had made a play for recently decided to get even with him—but good.

She invited him into her hotel bedroom and excused herself to "get into something more comfortable." He, too, made himself more comfortable by stripping completely in her bedroom. She then invited him into the bathroom on the pretense of having him shower with her.

Standing there in all of his glory, he pulled back the shower curtain. There was the entire crew, fully clothed, waiting for him in the tub.

The last laugh was theirs.

✈

Flying with captains who make informative PAs about points en route is always a special pleasure for the passengers. We were flying a DC10 trip from Los Angeles to Dallas/Ft. Worth with Jack Randall, a captain known for his abilities as an inflight commentator. We were over Phoenix when he picked up the microphone:

"Ladies and gentlemen, if you look out the windows on the left-hand side, you'll see the wonderful city of Phoenix, Arizona. Although I'm based in Chicago, this is my home when I'm not working.

"Now, if you count three major streets over on the left, and two streets down from the mountain range area, you'll see my house with the red Mercedes in front."

Two minutes had passed when the captain's now agitated Voice was heard again over the PA:

"Ladies and gentlemen, we'll be landing in fifteen minutes. I don't *have* a red Mercedes."

Upon routinely introducing ourselves to the cockpit crew, the captain handed us a typed itinerary of the service he expected to receive from us in flight: 9:05 was coffee #1, 10:15 was a soda water, 10:30 was coffee #2, 11:30 was lunch, and so on. The other cockpit crewmembers privately verified our initial opinion that it would be generous to define him as simply cocky and pompous. He was long overdue for having some of the wind knocked out of his sails.

After impatiently waiting to use the first-class lavatory for some time, the captain gave up and submitted to using the "peasant pots" in coach. He finished his business and then, with two feet of used toilet paper streaming out of the back of his pants, strutted all the way up to the cockpit.

The passengers were almost as impressed as we were.

The cockpit crew delights in having a little fun with the flight attendants, who, unfortunately, don't always realize when they're being had. It must be great fun if you're a passenger who's lucky enough to watch one of these little events unfold.

The cockpit of most airliners is located, of course, directly in front of the first-class section. The Boeing 747 is the exception: Its cockpit sits on top of the main deck of the airplane. Access to it and the upper-deck lounge is by a little spiral staircase at the rear of the first-class section.

Penny and Mary Ann were serving predeparture champagne to about thirty first-class passengers on an Allegiance

Airlines 747 flight from JFK to Los Angeles International (LAX). They had noticed a uniformed pilot board the aircraft carrying his two heavy flight kit bags. When he didn't go upstairs, but instead walked to the front of the first-class cabin, they assumed he must be a deadheading crewmember—just one more mouth to feed until he assumed active duty on a downline connecting flight.

As Penny started back up the aisle with champagne for a couple who had just taken their seats, she noticed the pilot now furiously feeling the forward bulkhead. He ran his hand up and down, back and forth on the carpeted wall, obviously searching for something. His actions had not gone unnoticed by most of the first-class passengers: He now held their undivided attention.

"Is there a problem? What are you looking for?" asked the confused flight attendant.

"The cockpit door!" replied the man, still feeling around on the solid wall.

"It's not down here. It's upstairs!" she exclaimed, her face becoming red with embarrassment for him.

"No, I *know* it's here somewhere!" he persisted.

She wanted to get this one out of the passengers' sight in a hurry. "Believe me, it's not!" she insisted in a strained whisper.

As she led him by the arm to the staircase, he winked at the perplexed passengers as he passed through the cabin and said, "Well, it damn sure was in the simulator."

✈

Most of us accept that while we are on duty our very souls are owned by the airline. Although we bid to work specific trips, we know that we are at the mercy of our company. They can reschedule us to work different flights if there are aircraft equipment positioning requirements, mechanical problems, or weather cancelations. Leastearn Airlines flight #311 was en route to Miami from New York's JFK airport when the unusual occurred.

"Miami center. Uh, Miami center," the captain radioed to the Miami air traffic control post. "This is Leastearn three-one-one. We are being hijacked. Repeat, we are being hijacked. Request vectoring for Havana." A few seconds passed and the captain continued, "Would you find out from crew scheduling if this constitutes a reassignment?"

They rarely lose their sense of humor!

Dick Williams is a captain who's always a pleasure to fly with. He's protective of his flight attendants—especially the younger ones who are just starting out on their very first jobs.

He'd flown several recent trips with a sweet, timid young woman who'd been teary-eyed each time he saw her. Something was troubling her greatly, and, having daughters of his own, he felt a responsibility to help. Overhearing a conversation between two other flight attendants, he suspected the problem was that the young, unmarried woman was going to have a baby.

Realizing it would be inappropriate for him to broach the subject with her, he decided to speak confidentially with her inflight supervisor after the trip terminated in New York. The supervisor was sympathetic and grateful for his candor, assuring him that she would look into the situation immediately. The captain thanked her, left the airport, and proceeded to make the two-hour journey to his home in Connecticut.

To say he received an icy reception from his wife would be an understatement. Seems she had intercepted the taped telephone message that said simply: "Captain Williams, you'll be happy to hear that the flight attendant is *not* pregnant."

It took three weeks of explanations, two dozen roses, and a call from the flight attendant's supervisor to calm the home front!

✈

A new flight attendant was being crucified by an overly demanding captain; he was calling every few minutes for something. A veteran flight attendant sympathized with this poor colleague and decided enough was enough. "Let me take care of that creep. He won't bother you again." When the captain called the next time wanting coffee, the older flight attendant dumped a heaping portion of powdered laxative into his drink.

It worked. The captain didn't bother her again: He was glued to the toilet seat for most of the remaining day.

Never mess with the hand that feeds you!

✈

When you're on "reserve" with an airline, you fly when they tell you to fly. Being unable to be contacted is a lesser offense than refusing or missing an assigned trip.

This captain gets an "A" for his creativity in avoiding an assignment. When crew scheduling woke him at 3 A.M. to assign him to a 5 A.M. departure, he passed the phone to his wife and said in a voice loud enough for them to hear on the other end, "Here, darling, I think it's someone calling for your husband."

Crew scheduling omitted the usual question and answer period.

Here is a springtime story from Greenwich, Connecticut.

Apparently the local hospitals have joked in print that they can always tell when spring has arrived because of the large number of airline pilots admitted with injuries sustained through yard work or home repair (though clumsy captains are not always at fault).

A pilot decided to patch his slate roof. Because work had to be done on the back side of it and the slate was very slippery, he tied a rope around his waist and fastened the other end over the roof, to the fender of his station wagon parked in the circular drive out front.

At dusk, when he was almost finished with the job, his wife hopped into the station wagon and hurriedly drove off to the grocery store. The handyman was pulled up the back side of the roof, down the front side, to the ground, and dragged for a block before a screaming neighbor was able to flag down the driver.

It took the doctors three days to remove all the gravel from the captain's bruised body.

We bet he doesn't do that again!

Another pilot may have had the same hospital room in Greenwich. It was springtime again, so this one decided to get out the chain saw and do a little pruning. He climbed high into an old oak tree, noticed a couple of branches that needed to come off, and the rest is surely a study in confusion: You see, he sawed the limb off on which he was sitting. From what his wife said, big bird damn near killed himself!

Allegiance Airlines DC10's feature a special television camera in the cockpit that enables passengers to view the take-off and landing from the pilot's perspective. For some cockpit crewmembers, it's showtime.

One captain we know put on a gorilla arm so that when he pushed the throttle forward during take-off, passengers would wonder just who or what was driving. It was even funnier after landing, when the passengers watched the co-pilot hand the arm a banana.

For some new engineers who aren't aware of this strange form of inflight entertainment, the camera can be embarrassing—especially when they're caught picking their noses.

The DC10-30 first-class galley was so tiny that each time a cockpit crewmember came out of the cage, it required a massive reshuffling of all the carts and catering set-ups.

After the engineer exited the pit for his tenth visit to the potty, the older galley flight attendant said to him, "Listen, son, the next time we fly together, would you consider wearing a catheter?"

He looked perplexed. "What would I need birth control for?"

A pilot was out for a moonlight drive with a stewardess whose heart he had been trying to win for quite a while. They had enjoyed a very romantic evening together, so he decided to park the car at the end of a dock to watch the ocean.

The night was going well; his confidence was high, the time was right to issue the invitation. "Honey, why don't just the two of us take off for the Bahamas tomorrow?" Overjoyed but very flustered when she said yes, he put the car in forward instead of reverse and drove it right into the bay.

We're sure his girlfriend would have preferred to fly.

The meal service was finished, and Liz had just completed the necessary inflight paperwork. As she prepared to do her routine cabin check, a puzzling announcement came from the cockpit:

"Ladies and gentlemen, it's odd but we seem to have lost our automatic pilot. If anyone has any information regarding this malfunction, please contact one of our flight attendants. Thank you!"

Knowing it was not common procedure to solicit mechanical advice from laymen or to inform passengers of a problem without first telling the flight attendants, Liz headed for the cockpit to see if all was okay.

She walked out of the galley and nearly stumbled over a 20-inch motorized robot wearing the captain's uniform cap, merrily wheeling its way down the aisle. Her expression of amazement was matched by those of forty passengers who had turned around in their seats to watch this strange creature proceed to the back of the airplane.

The "lost" auto pilot had been found, and he didn't even ask for a coffee refill!

Masterbase

NOTES ON "RESERVE"

Each airline has a principal fortress where all battle strategies are formulated. Corporate offices, centralized training facilities, a main reservations unit, and crew scheduling and planning are all usually located at "headquarters," which we fondly refer to as the "Masterbase" (the word has a sort of definitive ring to it). It's here that airline officials decide what color to paint the airplanes, whether the uniform buttons should have the airline logo on them, and whether removing one olive from your salad will truly save us $112,000 yearly. They will also decide whether or not you are the kind of person they want to do PR work for them at 35,000 feet.

If that is *your* wish, the first step is the INTERVIEW. The initial one is usually a group affair where you and forty other hopefuls all wearing blue suits and white blouses must convincingly argue that you don't want to be with your loved ones on holidays, that it is important to go all night without sleep, and that a large starting salary is not essential because you've always wanted to live out of your car, anyway. If you can somehow duplicate this performance during the following individual interviews, you'll be welcomed into the flight orphanage. Knowing what lies ahead for you brings back many memories for us.

Our first close encounter with the Masterbase came during our month-and-a-half venture at flight-attendant training school, The Charm Farm. Thinking we were there for sun, fun, and to learn tips on managing our new and carefree life-styles, we didn't give a second thought to the barbwire fence that surrounded the place, assuming it was there to keep "undesirables" from gaining access to this hallowed ground. Feeling a lot like Private Benjamin by the end of our first twenty-four hours, we revised that conclusion completely.

Since we'd be given a one-way ticket to report immediately to base after training, we all arrived with everything we owned. We were each awarded a yellow plastic name tag that we were required to wear at all times. To management and senior flight attendants passing through, it eloquently announced "I am stupid and have no idea what's going on; please laugh at me and treat me like a piece of excrement."

The complimentary cafeteria food was really delicious: corn fritters, bread, rice pudding, mashed potatoes, and a box of Niagara starch to snack on later in our rooms. Surviving on this diet taught us that it would be entirely possible to live cheaply once "on the line."

Roommate assignments were exciting. You didn't know if you'd get the crybaby, the prankster, the snitch, or the bitch. We got Miss Watermelon—an attractive moron who actually kept her rhinestone tiara on display in the room. She had such a difficult time understanding the material that more than once we worried that we were missing something important. We weren't; she was: a brain.

After the welcome announcements were made by several time-warped members of management (circa 1964), we were directed to stand in front of the cutthroat group and "tell about ourselves." Due to nervousness, some candidates volunteered unfortunate personal information that would later prove to be directly responsible for their invitations to leave training. "Oh, well, better them than me!" we each thought as we grimly wondered which of us would next be silently removed during the night to avoid upsetting the rest. It was like being in a nursing home watching your friends cross over one by one.

That was the only "real" part of an otherwise "simulated" six weeks. There were fuselage mock-ups, exit door mock-ups, galley mock-ups, cockpit mock-ups, interior mock-ups, entrée mock-ups (you'd never see the actual food look as good as that plastic stuff did), and makeup mock-ups—no, muck-ups.

Our "T and A" class (Technique and Application) was presided over by a reject of the 1928 "House of Beauty" who looked like she grew up in Transylvania—sans fangs. Well, that's not fair: She never smiled, so we can only guess. By the time she got finished with our faces, we could have worked any street corner in the world and been proud. She ushered several of our blotchy-skinned classmates to the medical department to confirm the "potential skin problem" that threatened to be their undoing (not that the mandatory 4 inches of cement smeared on their faces had any bearing on this condition at all).

"Always find the time during the flight to reapply your makeup, girls" was her number one law. Little did we know then that the only thing we would apply to our faces in flight would be a cold, wet washcloth to bring down our puffy eyes long enough for us to *see* during landing.

The emergency procedures classes were our favorites. The instructors gave us exact commands to start yelling for any given emergency. By then we needed to yell; and besides, it felt just like cheerleader tryouts. "Grab ankles! Get your heads down 'til the plane stops!" We decided then and there that "Grab ankles! Get your heads down, and kiss your ass good-bye" would have been more appropriate, but we kept our mouths *shut*.

There had been rules, rules, and more rules. Thank God Moses didn't get orders from these "higher authorities"— he'd still be on the mount waiting for them to be engraved in stone.

Transformation was nearly complete by the fifth week. We'd been measured for those wonderful official uniforms and were looking forward to four years of payroll deductions to pay for them. By this time we all looked like everybody else . . . who looked a lot like bald eagles. Management believed that there was a link between length of hair and rebelliousness. (Maybe there is, because now our hair is a lot longer than our patience.)

Graduation day arrived. In our eyes, our preview of hell was finally coming to a close. Training had been a six-week crapshoot. The gods had smiled upon us: We hadn't been whisked away by that limo that routinely ate unfortunate classmates and spit them out at the Dallas/Ft. Worth airport for the disappointing journey home. (Yes, yes, we're sorry you quit your previous job; and, now that you mention it, you *did* look better with the two feet of gorgeous golden blond hair we hacked off.)

The "Junior Birdman" award was given to the geek whom the instructors felt best personified the ultimate flight attendant. We called it the "Eddie Haskell Award" and were glad we had been nice to this person, who would surely fill the next management vacancy that opened up at The Farm.

Our wings were pinned on. We had survived basic training. The cage door was open: It was our turn to fly.

A large, Southwestern city is now home to Allegiance Airlines' corporate headquarters. All of the brilliant prime directives issue forth from centralized training there. Hence, our chapter title, Masterbase.

During initial training, we received an overview of some of the routes we'd be flying. We didn't know what we were getting into then, but we do now. The following is a brief explanation of some of our most consistently infamous trips:

1. S and M Flights—JFK/LAX. Otherwise known as "Stand and Model." You must learn to work around the actors and actresses who affect statuelike poses, draping themselves across seatbacks, on credenzas, by emergency-door handles, and so forth.

2. The Roach Coach—JFK/San Juan, Puerto Rico. The airplanes become so bug infested that after-trip uniform fumigation becomes necessary.

3. Kosher Klipper—JFK/Miami. Also known as the Bagel Bullet. Stories of the never-ending exodus to Miami originate here.

4. Miracle-Miles Flight—Miami/JFK. The boarding lounge of this flight usually looks like a wheelchair convention. For some inexplicable reason, upon landing in New York, all of these people have been miraculously cured: Not one passenger will need a wheelchair for deplaning. (They may even be strong enough by then to push you out of the way in the baggage-claim area.)

5. Red-Eye Flights—LAX/JFK. By the strange behavior exhibited by passengers on these all-nighters, you would think that the moon were full 365 days a year.

6. Up Chuck Truck—Anywhere/Nashville. Because of the hilly terrain, approach into Nashville is always bumpy. Even if you've made it to this point just fine, you're now in for the big heave-ho.

7. BM Flight (The Businessman's Run)—New York/Chicago. Silent, surly, newspaper-laden paper pushers, after grunting, groaning, and going to the bathroom, are amazingly transformed into smiling and talkative human beings after this two-hour flight.

After five weeks of touch and go, a prospective flight attendant had surprised herself by making it to the final week of training. It was time for her to perform the dreaded verbatim emergency evacuation drills for the training supervisors and the FAA inspectors. Knowing that she was a borderline case and probably wouldn't perform her drills correctly anyway, she got out of her jumpseat and decided to go for broke.

"Unfasten seatbelts! Come this way! Bring everything with you!" she shouted.

Bring everything with you? No, no, no . . . .

"That's right," she continued, making a great show of it. "I said bring it with you! Your furs, your diamonds, Momma's heirlooms—'cause they're gonna burn in this damn airplane!"

She was eighty-sixed, but she went out with a bang.

One wonders just who pays whom to keep juicy airline tidbits from gaining national media attention. The press would have loved this one. As in all major foul-ups in life, lots of things work in tandem to make a total mess of the situation. When these disasters occur in the industry, the very possibility that they may occur again results in a barrage of memos and initiation of new procedures.

Flight #307 was to leave LaGuardia at 2:45 P.M. to go to Chicago. The cabin crew and the flight deck crew were delayed inbound on two respective flights. At 2:25 P.M. it was time to board the passengers for the Chicago flight, and, since the FAA requires that at least one emergency-qualified flight attendant be on the airplane before the passengers come on board, crew scheduling sent a new reserve flight attendant downstairs from the crew lounge to do the honors. The inbound cabin crew would be arriving to relieve her so she could get to her 3:15 Toronto departure at the next gate.

While the agent pulled the tickets in the departure lounge, the little, lonely flight attendant welcomed the passengers on board. It was a very harried boarding of a rushed and exasperated full load. The cockpit crew, having just arrived, situated themselves and proceeded to perform their preflight duties. Wishing not to be disturbed by the total chaos in the cabin, they simply closed the cockpit door and got on with doing the necessary checklists and paperwork, and examining the pornographic photos hidden in the usual cockpit locations by the previous flight-deck crew.

All the reserve flight attendant knew was that she had welcomed the passengers, they were settled in and ready to go, and she had to get her butt onto the Toronto flight, which was to board in five minutes. She liked her brand-new job and wanted to keep it for a while, so she calmly gathered her things and went like a good little flight attendant to the next gate.

Meanwhile, the gate agent was frantically tallying boarding passes and tickets at the desk; all attentions were on avoiding a dreaded delay. He rushed to the aircraft when he finished, grabbed the PA microphone, and delivered the usual, "On behalf of the New York ground crew . . ." announcement poop. Shoving the paperwork in back of the jumpseat panel, he closed the airplane door, and the flight was ready to push back.

So it did. Since the cockpit indicator for open aircraft doors was off, the cockpit crew knew that all was A-OK.

The airplane made its way to the end of the runway with the crew wondering why the flight attendants were not considerate enough to offer them a cup of coffee, a lewd joke, or something—and they took off.

About thirty minutes into the flight, there was a timid knock on the cockpit door. Since no cockpit crew will open the door to a knock, they ignored it. The third time the knocking occurred, the engineer cautiously opened the door. A man very apologetically asked, "Excuse me, but how do we go about getting some coffee back here?"

There was NO CABIN CREW on board!!

It would have been terrible if there had been a decompression at 30,000 feet, a fire in the cabin, a need for an emergency evacuation, or (God forbid) a scheduled-dinner flight instead of a "peanut" one (wouldn't want to waste all that costly airline cuisine).

As a result of this fiasco, it is now required that agents personally hand the flight paperwork to a real, live flight attendant. Yes, the agent got the blame for that one, but we always have wondered how it never made it to the papers. Hmmm . . .

A flight attendant asked a "new hire" if she had been given the hula hoop test during the interview. She shook her head "no." He went on to tell her that airlines always give the test to make sure they get the right people. If the hoop won't fit over your head, you're Gamma material; if it stops at your boobs, Lonestar hires you; if it rests at your hips, you'll go with Divided; and if the hoop falls to the floor, you're welcomed to Allegiance.

We are more than a little paranoid about always having to put our best foot forward. In general, potentially serious inflight problems aren't usually too risky: Looking concerned about them *is*!

During a recent flight, severe turbulence resulted in the temporary loss of all our electrical power. As you can imagine, we had our hands full trying to perform safety checks and stow all catering equipment in the nearly dark, earthquake-like environment.

As fate would have it, a new flight service supervisor (whose only flight-related credential consisted of having been the chief uniform fitter) was on board doing a checkride on our crew. Would you believe that, after landing, she submitted official reports reprimanding all of us for "inappropriate facial expressions"?!

Smile and the world smiles with you.

Layovers
and Other
Fiascos

"Hmm . . . a dollar a room per night is the BEST you can do? Sorry, but that's still way over budget."

nd yet another luxurious would-be layover hotel slips by. Once again the airline layover contract has been awarded to the

"No-Tell Motel-Vacancy"—a family kind of place with av-ocado plastic curtains, telephones bolted to the nightstands, and beds that are chained to the floor. Shop and compare.

Okay, so they're not *all* that bad. It's just that the quality of our prearranged accommodations varies widely from city to city for no apparent reason. We suggest that, for the sake of consistency, all airlines pool their resources and just set up an airline crew trailer park somewhere between the air-port and the city's main landfill. We foresee no problems in assigning those with the lengthier layovers on-site house-keeping and maintenance duties.

Our main gear wheels have just touched down, heralding the end of our last flight segment for the day. Think back to the closing scenes from Act I of *Gone With the Wind* . . . to the heroine mercilessly whipping the steed that had served her so well in her desperate quest to return home to Tara. Thirsty, starving, exhausted, dripping thick white foam from his mouth, the poor beast finally collapses to the ground with a thud. As the last of you leaves the airplane, we know just how he felt.

It's time to remember where in *this* cabin we initially stashed our luggage. The company forbids us to check it like you do (there's a message in that, somewhere). Often, weather, mechanical problems, and so forth cause our itin-eraries to be changed more times than our underwear. We have to be prepared.

We put our luggage back on our little "wheelies" and, handicapped by these pull carts, begin our Flight Attendant Wheelie Special Olympics by negotiating the terminal obstacle course: out the narrow jetbridge doors; around a Japanese tour group and several wheelchairs; through a crawling, drooling Romper Room section; onto the moving sidewalk; down the escalator; to our off-the-curb limo pick-up point—where we find no limo in sight. We'll stand there until moss grows on us waiting for the van that has been instructed to delay our pick-up because we were late inbound. (The agent forgot to call them when we touched down. Thank you.)

Yes, the airline arranges for the crew's transportation, too. All tabs are paid directly by the company except our food and beverage ones. Expense money is allocated on a per-hour basis for our time away from home base and will be included in our end-of-month paychecks.

The specific requirements for all of our layover hotels are contractually negotiated between the flight crew unions and management: twenty-four-hour room service is a must, as are air conditioning and room-darkening blinds. Our union fought long and hard to win the right to layover hotel rooms that are padded. That way we receive no complaints of disturbing other people as we're slamming our heads against the walls after our trips.

It's amazing, but the moment we slide the room key into the latch, we're no longer tired. The race is on, and if you're the last one to the lounge for the "crew debrief," your penalty is to buy the first round of industrial strength cocktails. (There are the occasional "slam-clickers" who refuse to participate in our group activities. But if you camp out by the hallway ice machine, you'll soon spot them secretly filling their ice buckets as they prepare to do something even worse: drink *alone*.)

It's against regulations *ever* to drink in uniform, so your costume comes off first. After marginally unpacking and building your little layover nest, it's time to rinse your body. This is when having been on the line a while will really come in handy. Otherwise, you'll waste precious moments trying to figure out how to get the water to stay in *this* bathtub. (Through frustrating experience, we become so proficient in the operation of all novel bathtub fixtures that we could easily work as Kohler sales reps.)

As you enter the Neptune Bar to the jukebox accompaniment of either Waylon Jennings or Merle Haggard, you won't recognize your fellow crewmembers in "civies." (They're the clean-cut yet somehow sleazy-looking bunch at the corner table playing "Klondike.") Be careful: Happy hours have been known to get out of hand. On a Harlingen layover, you may wonder at four in the morning how the hell you've wound up in Tijuana. (Never mind your 7 A.M. departure.)

The Federal Aviation Administration regulations state that there is to be no drinking of alcoholic beverages by crewmembers within eight *hours* of a flight. Fine. Eight hours should be plenty of time for your body to metabolize two quarts of Jack Daniels. (A slightly looser crewmember interpretation of this regulation is, "No drinking within eight *feet* of an airplane.") Most crewmembers are, in fact, very conscientious about observing this regulation. After all, it's no fun going to work sweating wine. On an airplane, one working day with a hangover is lesson enough to encourage you to mend your ways.

Sometimes we end up making it to dinner. Occasionally, an extremely nice captain (with only one family to support) will pick up the tab for our whole gang. Most of the time it works best if we request separate checks. The reason for this is THE NEW FLIGHT ENGINEER. If we're all having salads, THE NEW FLIGHT ENGINEER will order a six-course dinner and insist that we just split the bill. If, however, we're all ordering steaks, he will order a salad and will make sure that he gets his own *separate* check. THE NEW FLIGHT ENGINEER will even be pissed-off if he's shorted 37 cents, so be cool. Be more than fair. Go the extra mile. I want to breathe in flight tomorrow (he's in charge of aircraft pressurization), and I would rather keep my eardrums intact during descent.

SEX BETWEEN CREWMEMBERS

There are three schools of thought on this issue:

1. Keep your personal and professional lives separate.

2. This is a very stressful job, and the importance of keeping your cockpit crew happy and relaxed cannot be overemphasized ("the life you save may be your own" philosophy).

3. None of this is anybody's damn business.

As far as we can tell, in the olden days most of the pilots were married, and all of the flight attendants were single (they had to be). So on layovers, they all went out, had a rollicking good time, and then paired off at the end of the evening.

However, in the old days, one flight attendant had compromised herself on a layover with a particular captain whom she had always found irresistible. On the following layover, he had definitely lost interest in her. Hell hath no fury . . . so she sneaked a red nightie of hers into his layover luggage hoping that the nightgown would be intercepted at the end by the captain's somewhat (!) possessive wife.

The captain discovered the garment during the flight and

decided to get the flight attendant but good. He approached her in the aisle of the 727 during her meal service to an all male first-class cabin. She was obviously horrified as he handed the red nightie to her in front of God and everybody and said coolly, "I think you left this in my room last night."

During times like those, we prayed for trapdoors. But things aren't the same *at all* anymore: Lots of the flight attendants are married, too . . .

It's time to go to sleep now. You've called the hotel operator for your wake-up call and set your fifteen alarm clocks for your "oh-dark-hundred" wake time. Be sure you take into account any pertinent time-zone changes, or you'll be sorry. There's really no reason to worry, anyway. You'll usually wake up because nine out of ten layover hotels are on the direct approach path to the airport. Sleeping through what sounds like a buzz-bomb attack is unlikely—unless you were raised on an aircraft carrier (some of us were).

Your internal clock will become very efficient after you are wakened once or twice by the captain calling from the lobby wondering (with the rest of us in the van) where you *are*. You'll be so panicked and confused that you'll brush your teeth four separate times and wonder why it seems that when you're in a great hurry, it takes *forever* to get ready. That will also be the morning that you'll need to jump start your dying hair dryer. Just pray that you can find the lobby *fast*.

When your layover isn't so short, you'll want to experience the local culture. First, you'll need to find out where you are. Open the top drawer of the nightstand and take out the book with the white bell on it that says *AT&T* at the

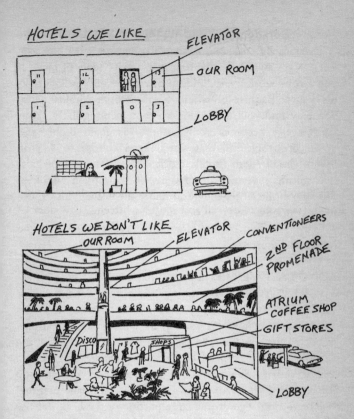

HOTELS WE LIKE

ELEVATOR
OUR ROOM
LOBBY

HOTELS WE DON'T LIKE

OUR ROOM
ELEVATOR
CONVENTIONEERS
2ND FLOOR PROMENADE
ATRIUM
COFFEE SHOP
GIFT STORES
Disco
SHOPS
LOBBY

top. Halfway down, there's a city name. Voila! Mystery solved.

In the light of day, you will walk joyously outside, thrilled that you are doing what you told the interviewer you wanted to be doing when you applied for this job: You are "traveling." Only it's weird here and not like you imagined at all, and you're confused because you didn't think the 747 was capable of leaving the solar system.

Trips are awarded according to seniority (date of hire). If you bid to work a trip, and no one senior to you wants it, it's yours. Because of where your seniority "holds" you, you may find you're working the same trip regularly. Your layover city becomes your home away from home, and you'll probably find that you'll even choose to stay in "your" hotel room (hotels block off the same set of "airline" rooms repeatedly). We know of one captain who kept a six-pack (for emergency use) under the bed in "his" room for six months, with no one drinking or removing it.

Crew planning ensures that some layovers are long and others are short.

LONG LAYOVER (Example):   10 hours in Dayton.
SHORT LAYOVER (Example):   36 hours in Paris.

International layovers present us with great recreational opportunities. You can have fun in the sun on a Caribbean island (you'll be shipped home free of charge in a Brown and Serve bag when you die of sunstroke), or you can shop 'til you drop in Europe (*the* great flight-attendant pastime) where you can also drop a large portion of the U.S. defense budget just for dinner. You really should opt for Europe . . . you haven't lived until you've seen Bugs Bunny cartoons dubbed in French or done your morning aerobic workout to the accompaniment of a traditional oom-pah band.

International travel comes with all sorts of benefits: Time will seem to stand still (you won't even know today's date), and you'll feel totally carefree (you won't remember your name).

This is how to turn your hair dryer into a blowtorch:

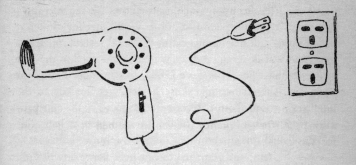

You can cook in your room and save money.

After a long airline career, it *is* true that you'll feel at home in hundreds of cities . . . you'll even know which nightstand drawers the Gideons missed.

One final note: We promised our fellow flight attendants that we'd clarify for you the difference between a "layover" and a "stopover." *We* have layovers—overnight stays in cities away from our homes during our working trips. *You* have stopovers—periods of time in an intermediate airport before you reach your final destination.

We can all breathe easier now.

Most of the cockpit crewmembers are really great guys (*and* girls now—some at Leastearn are even girls who used to be great guys). Whatever their gender, they love a good joke, but sometimes our initiation pranks don't quite turn out as we intend.

Once the crew decided to have a little fun with the new flight engineer, so upon reaching the hotel for the evening's layover, we set our plan in motion. We all met for dinner at about seven and decided to eat in the hotel restaurant. Conversation was flowing, and we were all engrossed in the war stories being told. This gave Linda, our number one flight attendant, the chance to excuse herself, get the key to the engineer's room from the cooperative front desk, and proceed to stitch up the ends of his uniform trouser legs. She accomplished this in about ten minutes, rehung them just as she found them, and returned to our little party downstairs.

Since we had a scheduled 6:05 A.M. limo pick-up to the airport the next morning, most of us had put in for a 5:00 A.M. wake-up call. So, of course, had the engineer. But the captain, who was also in cahoots with us, called the hotel operator late that night and rescheduled the engineer's wake-up call from 5:00 to *6:00,* giving the poor fool five minutes to dress and get to the lobby. We hardly could wait until morning!

By about 6:00 A.M., the entire flight crew was in the lobby waiting with anticipation not unlike that of the coyote for the road runner. We continued to wait. No engineer. Then we heard the front desk page our captain. He picked up the house phone, and we all watched as his expression changed from one of total mirth to sick panic.

Seems that all our plans came off perfectly—except for one thing. The engineer had overslept all right, and in his great hurry to get ready, he'd made some rather athletic moves in thrusting his legs into his pants. Expecting to find the floor at the bottom of his trouser legs, he wasn't at all prepared for the potato sacks we'd left him with. In his haste, the klutz had lost his balance and broken his ankle. (It was amazing he hadn't broken his neck!)

Because we were at a little outstation, the company had to deadhead in a new flight engineer. As we could go nowhere in our plane without an engineer, our outbound flight was canceled that morning. We were all more than a little afraid that our careers would be, too, but the engineer never said a word to management about how he really broke his ankle. Now that's a good sport!

The flight crew rarely misses a chance to have a lot of fun with each other. Once, after getting hotel room keys in the Salt Lake City Hilton, the head flight attendant, Sandy, got into the elevator with the flight engineer and about seven devout Mormon women who were on their way to the top-floor restaurant. Sandy's room was on the second floor, and when she got out, she turned and screamed to the poor flight engineer who was left in the elevator, "I'm not afraid to report you to professional standards. Don't you *ever* touch me there again!"

The doors closed and we're sure the engineer's ride with the solemn women to his room on the twentieth floor was a pleasant one. He's probably still plotting to get even with Sandy.

The flight attendants were thoroughly disgusted. Every time they got to the hotel in Frankfurt after an all-night flight, they had to wait for their rooms to be readied. After two months, they decided to fix the hotel. As soon as they arrived, they all changed into their pajamas and sat in the lobby.

From that day on, their rooms were ready and waiting for them.

One hotel extended a special service to Allegiance Airlines flight crews by getting security clearance for the courtesy van to drive us directly to our airport operations area at Los Angeles International. This way we could drive on the airport ramp, saving us the trouble of schlepping a great distance from the front of the terminal to our airplane.

During this ride, however, we had a brand-new limo driver who got royally lost and drove around every taxiway possible. We felt we were in a remake of the Keystone Kops, and knew it wouldn't get any worse after we found ourselves nose to nose with a 747 at the end of the runway.

"Oops, I think we're in the wrong place," was all the flustered driver could manage.

A pilot met a beautiful young woman during a San Francisco layover. Late that evening, after the two of them managed to get totally trashed, he accompanied her back to her apartment. In the middle of the night nature called, and still very much asleep, he opened up a door that he thought led to the bathroom. As he began waking up, the horrified pilot found himself halfway down the apartment building hall in his birthday suit.

Two major problems faced him: He didn't know the woman's last name, and he had no idea which apartment was hers. He eventually enlisted the help of a somewhat bewildered doorman in locating his phantom date.

It's no secret that French people don't always care for Americans. They tend to be a bit, shall we say, condescending.

Marty wanted to explore Paris on one particular trip, so he asked the concierge, "May I have a subway map, please?"

"Well, what city do you want?" the concierge demanded arrogantly.

"Oh, Brooklyn, of course," Marty answered, and walked off.

Airlines are all pretty touchy about weight restrictions—not only as they apply to cargo loads. Flight attendants must weigh-in between specific minimums and maximums on a company-prescribed weight chart. There's no such thing as "weight in proportion to height"—and they're serious about it. If it's noticed that you seem to be spreading a little too much, it's likely you'll be put on dreaded "weight check" by your supervisor. That makes it mandatory for you to come in and be weighed regularly until you're once again emaciated. It's a humiliating experience.

A newly hired flight attendant had a layover in Dallas. She'd put on a few pounds since she started flying; and, considering the prospect of being put on weight check, decided she'd better do something to remedy her appetite problem. So she bought some of those pills that are supposed to make you feel full after you have about three bites to eat, and before dinner that night, popped a couple.

The crew decided to introduce her to Mexican food. As she sat shoveling in chips and salsa, she realized that the pills weren't working too well, so she popped another two.

Halfway through her beans and rice, she fell back into her

chair, eyes rolling like one of those Macy's Parade inflatables. The pills had worked all at once, and she felt as though her body was being blown up by a bicycle pump.

When she rolled into her room later, she was thankful she had several hours before the next flight. She should have been. At altitude she would have exploded.

Splash

They *look* similar, but:

This object can swim.

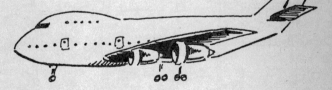

This object cannot.

▌t is an important distinction to consider before you decide to become an international crewmember or passenger. After thinking the matter through thoroughly, we decided to go for it. You should, too. Here's why.

During international training, we learned that, luckily, someone had the foresight to substitute automatically inflatable slide/liferafts for regular door-evacuation slides on "over-water-equipped" widebody airplanes. If you're taking a lengthy overwater flight, you'll be on one of these specially equipped airplanes. They differ from their domestic cousins in that they are outfitted with life vests, life rafts, and an international crew that has been trained to make Gilligan's Island a reality if need be.

These little flight interruptions can be a nuisance if you let them get you down. But, THINK POSITIVELY! Only *you* can make this a life-enriching experience. Here we go!

Your life vest is located in a pouch under your seat—along with seventeen wads of chewed Juicy Fruit. Remove it from the pouch and take it out of the clear, plastic bag. The thing is yellow, and it looks like this:

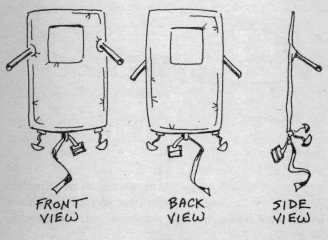

FRONT
VIEW

BACK
VIEW

SIDE
VIEW

We're going to demonstrate in the aisles how to use it. It took us four days of training to learn how to get into and out of it, so you'd better pay attention; but you won't—you'll be fumbling with it. By the time you give up, we'll be long gone performing other duties.

Why, you will wonder, did they not print *Front, Back,* or *This side up* on the device to cut down on the confusion of these four hundred people? Because, there *is* no front or back—just poke your head through the hole, wrap the strap around your waist, fasten, and tighten it until you feel like throwing up. You have donned your life vest properly. But DON'T INFLATE YET. You'd be like the Michelin man walking through the airplane aisles.

This entire event will be a special treat for all of you single people out there. Airlines instruct us to assign a male passenger to each female one. It's just like a square dance; and if you don't like your date, you can ditch him/her later.

After our "swan dive," the first thing we're told to do is to verify that "our" door exit is usable, in other words, above the water line. (Our instructors informed us that seeing fish lips or having a bird's-eye view of the *Titanic* through the porthole is a good indication that "it is not." Their omission of a contingency plan in the event of fish sightings by all crewmembers did not go unnoticed by us.)

If our exit is usable, we will open the doors in the emergency mode causing our little boats to puff up. You'll inflate your life vests, pile into the rafts, sit down, and put on your sunglasses. (Don't worry. You can repurchase duty-free items on the way home.)

These rafts have packed in their "floors" everything you'd need for a summer camping expedition: flares, drinking-water cans, hand pumps, whistles (the atmosphere will be a FESTIVE one), bailing buckets, shark repellent, fishing poles, suntan oil, and a copy of *Robinson Crusoe*. The fact that we'll have to move you and seventy-one other people out of the way first to get to them, should be of no concern. Whatsoever. Really.

The object being to stay afloat, at this point it will become increasingly important to think about cutting the raft away from the sinking aircraft. Failure to do so will probably mean the evening clambake is canceled.

Although the initial ordeal is over, we must position our six rafts (three from each side of the airplane) as closely to each other as possible and attempt to tie ourselves together. We have no oars, but *we* believe that 140 dog-paddling hands should be more than adequate to maneuver in open seas.

We made it! See, that was easy. As much fun as Disney World, and a fuller experience than even Outward Bound. And all for one all-inclusive ticket price.

On take-off, a DC10 lost power and proceeded to go straight into the sewage bay at the end of the San Juan runway. The crew deployed the slide/rafts and evacuated the aircraft according to procedure.

The funny part was that all those people floating in the stinky bay were picked up and brought back to the land by local fishermen in their boats. What in the world were they fishing for? (Be very careful eating Caribbean seafood.)

Aircraft #284 was the plane that was dumped via that aborted take-off. We chuckled when noticing that on the elevator doors in the lower galley, another flight attendant had printed in big, black letters, *Swamp Queen*.

The choicest flying assignments with our airline always go to the international divisions. There *is* much to commend Paris layovers. Most of the flight attendants who work these trips have at least fifteen years with the company. Unfortunately, as their seniority increases, so, inevitably, does their weight.

Our international or "across the pond" trips go so senior that there is now a standing joke among those of us in the company. Uniforms come in four sizes: small, medium, large, and international!

✈

Steve was working his first trip on international and was a bit apprehensive. He had heard that the international flight attendants were a tightly knit group so he felt the need to make a very good first impression. He was making mental notes as each flight attendant got on board. Checking names, he found his working partner was affectionately greeted by the other crewmembers as Ola.

As Steve worked the liquor cart, he was pleased with himself for remembering her name. He would smile and say, "Ola, would you please pass me a Coke?" "Ola, do you have any extra peanuts?"

She finally stopped in the middle of the aisle and said, "Steve, how come you keep saying 'hello' before asking me for something? You can just say, 'Juanita pass me . . .'"

Steve wanted to die. He thought he was making a good first impression!

✈

Donna, infamous at Allegiance for being her daddy's spoiled little princess, decided to go to Dallas for international training. She believed that the European flights would be so glamorous that she probably wouldn't even get her nails dirty. She wasn't quite prepared for training or, should we say, training wasn't prepared for her.

One of the tasks flight attendants must complete during "ditching" instruction is to jump out of an airplane mock-up into a pond and set up the raft from start to finish. It's a serious drill that is physically and mentally demanding.

Donna made her grand entrance into the class with sunglasses and life vest, a matching shower cap, and a pair of white gloves. She was slathered in suntan lotion—all she needed was a deck chair. She looked around the room at her astounded classmates, then turned to the instructors and said, "Well, I understand we're going on a little cruise today. I'm ready."

The international division will never be the same!

✈

Our foreign-born flight attendants are extremely careful to keep their passports with them whenever there's a chance that they would have to produce them for U.S. Immigration types.

After a long day at international training in Dallas, we were all debating where to have dinner that evening. Deciding we were in the mood for some good Tex-Mex food and a couple of margueritas, we announced to Heinrick, a new German-speaking flight attendant, that we would all go the South of the Border.

He became very serious as he asked in a very thick accent, "I do need pass-a-port?!?"

We all roared.

No, Heinrick, no "pass-a-port" needed.

✈

One scheduled trip was a thirty-seven minute (wheels up to wheels down) flight from San Juan to Santo Domingo on a full DC10. With three hundred passengers and a very short flight time, we walked down the aisles offering only trays of soft drinks.

The flight attendant approached a row of passengers with the beverage tray and said, "Would you like a Coke or a Sprite?"

"Well, which is the Coke and which is the Sprite?"

The other flight attendants in the aisle died laughing when they heard her say sweetly, "I don't know. I wasn't there when they poured them."

Star Wars

Although while we're off duty a chance encounter between crewmembers from competing companies is usually a welcome one, when we're at work, the cut-throat philosophy is operable more often than not. Deregulation is, in large measure, responsible for that. Competition is stiff; there's just too much at stake now.

Each carrier perceives itself as having a distinct personality, and the employees tend to mirror, even unconsciously, the competitive spirit of their managements. No opportunity to define the pecking order is passed by, whether it's vying for favorable pushback, take-off, or approach clearances, or getting served first in an airport coffee shop (as we play with our Tinker Toys).

As much as we may be hard-pressed to admit it, airline company loyalty runs deep. It's been drilled into our heads for so long that we're team players, that it's a logical step to assume there must be opposing teams. We're always looking for ways to outdo each other, some subtle and some not so subtle.

We suppose a bit of this is to be expected among people who are fairly strong willed and competitive by nature. The pilots get to excel in this department mainly because their direct encounters with other carriers (via radio) are numerous. For example, referring to take-off sequencing, the tower radioed: "Ah, Allegiance, you're number one."

"And that's just how it *should* be!" the cowboys in Allegiance's cockpit responded.

Word is, the skies are not quite as friendly as you may think—at least not from an insider's vantage point. Fortunately, airlines don't carry onboard weapons systems. Usually, verbal abuse will suffice, but sometimes . . . PLAY BALL!

Deregulation is, of course, good for you, the traveling public (as far as your wallets are concerned). It does, however, cause more friction than ever before among the competing flight crews.

One afternoon, a Gamma and a Leastearn jet were sitting side by side on the run-up pad at LaGuardia Airport, each awaiting a long overdue take-off clearance. The Gamma captain decided to have a little fun with the Leastearn crew in the cockpit of the 727 that was alongside Gamma.

"Ladies and gentlemen," the Gamma captain began over the onboard PA system. "In this climate of deregulation and dog-eat-dog competition, you'll be glad to know that the flight crews still maintain an excellent rapport with all of their sisters and brothers of the sky. Just to show you that feelings of friendliness and mutual respect still exist, we're going to radio over to the Leastearn cockpit and ask them to wave a big, friendly hello to us, so have a look out of our right-hand-side windows."

With that, unbeknown to the passengers, the Gamma co-pilot seated in the right-hand seat in the cockpit opened his window, stuck his right hand out, and proceeded to shoot the Leastearn captain the vulgar "bird" hand signal. The Leastearn captain was appropriately insulted, so he opened the window and, to the astonishment of the Gamma passengers eagerly awaiting a friendly, professional greeting, stuck his left arm out of the cockpit and gave them a real solid "up yours" elbow maneuver. Not the best PR move that Leastearn ever made . . .

Yep. One great, big happy family.

When an aircraft leaves the hangar to begin its originating trip of the day, maintenance routinely removes the gear pins. These pins (which are about four inches long and less than half an inch in diameter and have long red flags or streamers attached to them) externally lock the gear in the "down" position, preventing an inadvertant collapse while the airplane is on the ground. The pins must be removed before flight, since they also prevent the gear from being retracted once the plane is airborne. Confirming the absence of these pins is one of the several important checks the flight engineer routinely performs during the preflight "walk-around" of the aircraft.

While airplanes are still on the ground before being sequenced for take-off, radio communication is established through a common ground-control frequency—sort of a party line for all aircraft and ground controllers. This frequency, of course, would not be the most prudent selection for those wishing to discuss matters of a rather sensitive nature. For that kind of exchange, you would want to switch to the discreet company (airline) frequency.

The following friendly conversation between a close-to-the-runway Gamma L1011 and an Earthquake Airline 727 was relayed by one of our cockpit crews.

"Gamma ninety, this is Earthquake nineteen-sixty-seven. What is your company frequency, please? . . . Ah, Gamma ninety, this is Earthquake nineteen-sixty-seven. What is your company frequency? We'd like to talk to you for a minute."

"Earthquake nineteen-sixty-seven, we are the Gamma Perfectionists, and we do *not* use the company frequency for frivolous conversations."

After a few moments of silence for what was surely an Earthquake cockpit discussion, Earthquake continued for the listening ears of three hundred–plus pilots and controllers.

"Ground control, this is Earthquake nineteen-sixty-seven.

Would *you* please tell the 'Gamma Perfectionists' in Gamma ninety that their gear pins are still in!!"

Ouch.

Little Air Equator shared the terminal with big brother Allegiance Airlines at JFK. One afternoon, Air Equator was short ticket agents so the AA agents assisted.

As they began checking passengers' luggage in the Air Equator lines, the agents asked where the scales were. Luggage and cargo weights are important in assessing gross weight and balance measurements so the pilots can determine safe take-off and flight-plan specifications.

"Oh, we don't weigh any of that stuff. 707's are very forgiving airplanes."

The Allegiance agent was staring in disbelief. "But how do you know when it's full?"

"Well, that's easy. We know it's full when we can't shut the cargo doors."

Considering the weights of those airplanes, we bet they're pruning treetops all the way to Chile.

We should count our blessings living in America.

On an Airoflop flight from Moscow to Leningrad, the flight attendants all looked as if they could have starred in that hamburger commercial featuring the "Svimwear, eveningvear" fashion show. If you haven't seen it, suffice it to say that they were a bit unclean and beaten with the ugly stick.

The juice service began, and as the flight attendants served one row forward of where we sat, they stopped, went back to the first couple of rows to collect the glasses, went to the galley, filled the glasses (without washing them), and continued serving the next row.

So, folks, don't ever complain about our domestic carriers.

GETTING
THERE

THE STEWARDESS PROMISE

On my honor I will try:
To do my demo without ever laughing,
To help other creatures endure this flight,
To obey the FAA.

So you've decided there's no way around it . . . you have to
fly somewhere. We understand that the fun begins when
you start comparing fares.

The day of the week and the time of the day you wish to
travel, along with how far in advance you're willing to
cough up cash for the experience, all have lots to do with
how resentful paying for your ticket will make you.

If you choose to go on an all–nighter, or "red-eye,"
flight, for example, your ticket cost will be substantially
lower. This is due to three reasons:

1. You pay for a slightly less alert (these are weird hours for
us, too) flight deck and cabin crew.

2. You presumably will sleep some, thereby negating any
positive effects the cockpit crew may have derived from

your mental efforts at helping them maintain safety and control of the aircraft. (If you know what we're talking about here, you're one of those thirteen out of every ten passengers who is afraid of flying at least to some extent: digging your fingers into the armrests to hold the airplane together, leaning left or right in your seat to help us steer and maintain balance, keeping a vigilant watch out for other aircraft in the area to avoid a midair collision, and not moving a muscle during turbulence, thereby helping the little airplane to calm down.)

3. The flight is uncrowded owing to the SMART PEOPLE who opted not to fly at this time because of reasons 1 and 2.

There *is* a great variety of fares available today, but you already know this if money is of any consideration to you. Only a few seats are available on every flight at those tremendous saver fares that you hear so much about. To whom those tickets are sold is left totally to the discretion of the reservation agent, so have your pitiful story ready for the agent when you phone in. (For the best sob stories ever, we suggest you view *Queen for a Day* reruns.)

Do go ahead and tell everyone about your low, low fare while in flight. Fellow passengers and the flight crew-members will interact with you with approximately the same amount of warmth, kindness, and just plain old-fashioned courtesy they would show a leper with bad breath.

Although you're at least off to a good start if you've reserved a ticket, you're not finished yet. We thought you'd appreciate knowing up front about some other costs of air travel.

SOME OTHER COSTS

Your ticket price entitles you to seated transportation to your (sometimes) chosen destination, one brief lavatory visit, seven seconds of aisle leg-stretch time, a half-can of dog food, a soft drink, and, unless the airline is really being chintzy, all the O_2 you can breathe. Everything else is extra. For example:

$ 4   This is your headset rental fee. (Overheard on a DC10 JFK/LAX flight: "Miss, I just can't believe that even the headset is not included in the price of the ticket." "Sir, when you go to the movies, do they give you an airline ticket?")

$ 18   Drinks are $3 each. Contrary to popular opinion, if you're conscious, you can have another one. This cocktail charge reflects average amounts of alcohol necessary to calm you during light to moderate turbulence. If experiencing severe turbulence, multiply charge by three.

$ 5   Bring your own reading material unless you enjoy *Farm Machinery Today*, *Field Guide to the Berries of North America*, and *My Friend, the Bunny Rabbit*.

$ 35   We can't please everyone. This is the approximate cost for a full body sweater or, alternately, a battery powered "port-a-fan."

$ 85   Medical visit resulting from ingestion of foreign objects, bodily injury due to aisle meal cart roller derby, or the ever popular "Coffee-in-Crotch" caper.

$300   After your luggage-destroying trip out, you'll have to buy something in which to bring what's left of your belongings home.

$ 25   Toiletries for the time until we locate your luggage.

$ 90   Hotel/dinner costs due to weather-related cancellation. You have a 50 percent chance of omitting this expense.

$200   A conservative estimate. We're banking on the fact that you were a reasonably well adjusted individual to begin with, so two psychiatric sessions should be enough to put you on the road to recovery.

$762   TOTAL (This is exclusive of any legal fees you may incur.)

When you arrive at the airport, you'll be crazed already. Once again you've managed to drive the entire scenic journey behind a concrete mixer. The convenient curbside luggage checkpoints are closed because, as usual, the baggage handlers and porters are on strike. Pushing and kicking your five suitcases in front of you like a collie herding sheep, you proceed to the main ticket lobby where you're faced with the kind of dilemma that promises to make this trip consistent with all of your other ones. There are two, forty-five-body-deep lines, respectively labeled *Passengers Holding Tickets* and *Purchase Tickets Here*. You have already prepurchased your ticket over the phone, but you're not exactly holding it. This is what taking a multiple-choice test feels like to a schizophrenic. We're looking at a no-win scenario. (The correct choice is the *Purchase Tickets Here* line in this case.)

After studying the man's neck in front of you for what seems like three days, you finally retrieve the two flimsy bits of carbon paper worth over $600 that entitle you to suffer several hours of abuse (real or imagined) at the hands of those friendly, special people who live to get you there.

We're on board fifty minutes before departure getting everything ready for you. We stow our luggage, check all emergency equipment, test our PA microphones and video machines, organize the headsets for preflight rentals, open closets and overhead bins, obtain the enroute information from the cockpit crew, and set up all items for our initial beverage service. And you thought we came on board five minutes before you!

Are you traveling first or coach? First class is like Babylon: It's characterized by a luxurious, pleasure-seeking, and often immoral way of life. It's also serviced by inflight concubines. Do *you* want to be a party to *this*?

No, we thought not. Don't worry. We'll have fun in the back end. The fact that you'll have to be a contortionist to reach the personal items you have stowed under your seat before take-off need be of no concern to you. A flight attendant should be along in a couple of hours, and she'll be happy to retrieve that little vial of insulin for you then.

Does the inflight service perplex you? Beverages? A meal? Beverages with a meal? You'd really like to know what the sequence of events will be, but you're a nice person, so you'll just sit there, ask no questions, and take what you get. It may seem confusing, but it's all done according to a standard formula. Ask the gate agent initially if there *is* a meal scheduled for your flight. If the flight's under two and one-half hours, you'll usually get a one-shot deal—food and beverages are always served together. If it's over two and one-half hours and the flight departs before 9:00 A.M., you'll get the breakfast and beverage service first, and then a follow-on beverage service about an hour before you land. If a lunch or dinner is scheduled, the cocktail service comes first, then the dinner and beverages follow. See, it's easy. There's nothing left to chance. No "if the spirit moves us" on our part.

Flying will make your insides expand. You've probably noticed that after a long flight, your ankles are as big as your knees. After a three-day trip, we're so bloated we feel like we've eaten a football team. We guess it's fun for us "non-full-figured" girls; we do end up with tits for a day.

Working on an airplane develops great coordination and balance. Can *you* pour a cup of coffee when the floor, walls, and ceiling are heaving several feet at a time? It's like being Dale Evans, only without the fringe. Turbulence is so normal to us that sometimes we don't even notice when it gets really bumpy. We do hope that if we're ever at home during an earthquake, we'll have sense enough to know we're in danger.

Our flexibility regarding the onboard climate probably

accounts for why we seem so unresponsive to your requests. It's always either arctic or hotter than Death Valley. With a little experience, we learn to ignore it.

Do we ever get bored on a flight? Sometimes, when you are all sleeping or watching the inflight movie. But we always think of something clever and useful to do. Did you know that the toilet flush mechanism on a Boeing 767 creates 75 MPH of suction? It's fun to unroll toilet tissue all the way from the back lavatory up to the first class and then flush. That paper gets sucked up so fast it's like watching the dragon at Chinese New Year. Of course, it makes you think twice about sitting there naked. Makes you want to flush and RUN.

You do provide a lot of inflight entertainment for us though, even if it's unintentional. The Boomerang Effect is always pretty funny to watch. That's when you have your seatbelt or headset on and nature calls without warning. All efforts are in getting to that potty fast until you're snapped back into your seat like a rubber band. Take the headset off. Unfasten the seatbelt . . .

Okay. It's now showtime. Grab your bag, and let's try to find the plane.

A TYPICAL DAY AT THE AIRPORT

1. Your flight is departing from terminal 1, gate 13. On your mark, get set, GO!

2. Your flight is delayed one hour because we can't locate the captain. (He's about to be the all-time highest scorer on the "Nuke the Puke" video game in the employees' cafeteria.)

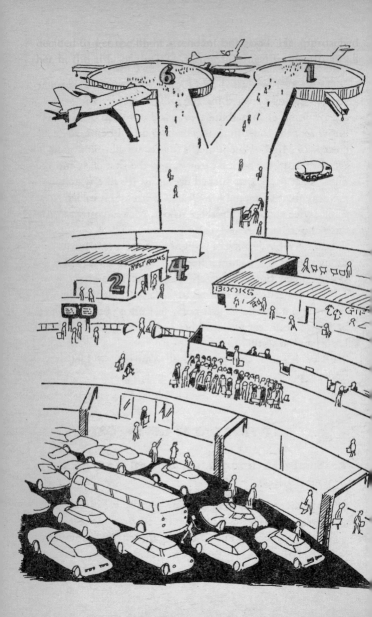

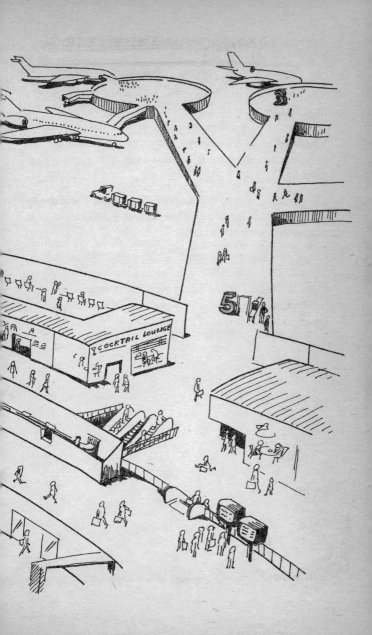

3. Your flight has been moved to depart from terminal 2, gate 40.

4. Uh-oh. The flight is oversold, and you weren't in the immediate gate area long enough in advance (two days) to guarantee yourself a reserved seat. But that's okay because there's another departure to your destination scheduled to leave in fifteen minutes from terminal 2 (where you are!), gate 34. Nature calls. You run fast like a bunny.

5. Intermediate stop to exchange "School Daze" pictures of your kids with the security checkpoint guard, with whom you are now intimate.

6. Oops, that flight is canceled. We're going to send it over to terminal 1, gate 12, instead to make it our Chicago flight. (You and thirty others were the only ones going to Dayton—can you really *blame* us? We're running a business here.)

The Cuckoo
Flew into
Our Nest

Getting to the airport, especially in major cities, is no small feat in itself. But compared with what comes next, it hardly deserves mention.

First, you stand in the "Attention K-mart shoppers" line for forty-five minutes so that you can have your luggage slammed on the moving belt behind the ticket counter. It's then sent down the chute into the River Styx, where the gods of the underworld decide its fate.

Most airlines hire celibate but highly virile (i.e., horny) gorillas as baggage handlers, so choosing sturdy luggage is imperative. You will want some that can withstand the daily rigors of flying. On the down side, no such luggage exists. (Airline travel reduces all bags to their lowest common denominator, so investing large sums in this category is sheer folly.)

Now the event begins. First, luggage is separated into soft-side, solid-molded, and cardboard-box categories. The soft-side luggage is taken to the Razor Room where each piece is catapulted at 50 MPH toward a wall-mounted 6- by 6-foot square of Yubangi tribe spearheads. Twice. The solid-molded is subjected to abuse by whatever piece of misshipped farm equipment is presently available. All cardboard boxes are sent to the Rain Room, where they are steamed until their dimensions change noticeably.

The luggage is then ready for the ramp baggage train, where the object is to shake the pieces off the little trucks at top speed. (Extra points are awarded if the fallen piece is in the direct path of a taxiing 747.) Next, the belt loader chews your luggage and spits it out in the (wet) belly of the airplane.

Basically, the same process occurs in reverse when the bags arrive at your destination. *If* the bags arrive at your destination. If the bags arrive at your destination *during* your stay there. Otherwise, they are pummeled at another location.

That's the only explanation we can come up with. Looking at luggage remnants at the other end, we find it inconceivable that baggage suffers this sort of mutilation simply from being put on and taken off of an airplane. We suggest that the best way to cope with the possibility of luggage destruction is to avoid having any sort of identifying information on it. That way, if you did recognize what was left of your case, you could ignore it, walk away, and declare it M.I.A.

After you've checked and abandoned your luggage, it's time for the ever popular security checkpoint game, where they try to decide if you are related to Norman Bates. Unfortunately, a couple of people have ruined it for all of us, so be careful not to inquire how Cuba's weather is this time of year or to suggest that you'd really like to pick up some nice cigars for Father's Day.

You'll probably feel some sense of vindictive satisfaction (admit it) to learn that all flight crewmembers must pass through these checkpoints, too. That's okay once or even twice a day, but when we work five trips daily and go through these machines as many times, we halfway expect to see skeleton outlines faintly showing through our uniforms. We're sure our purses already glow in the dark. (You know, if the company would agree to metal-coat the fabric of our uniforms, it could be a fun aid to help you guess our age and seniority. The more times through the machine, the clearer our X-ray—sort of a carbon-dating system for flight attendants.)

You've made your way to the gate, and now the real show begins with an announcement by the agent that soon you will be privileged to fight your way into the machine.

The boarding announcement is made . . . "Will all passengers seated in rows 35 to 40 please board at this time." Out of a plane of 300, don't you find it odd that 275 people get up to board? If they are all confused about their seats at this point, imagine what they are like once they are on the plane!

The trampled boarding flight attendants (we call them "pluckers and stuffers" because they "pluck" your tickets and "stuff" you in the bird) feel something like live bait thrown into a piranha tank. The way people push and shove, you would think we were boarding the last dinghy of the sinking *Titanic.*

Next comes the jetbridge line-up phase, where the temperature is guaranteed to be either a toasty 100 degrees or a brisk 17. You'll probably never have to endure a boring median temperature. It just doesn't work that way.

We do our best to set the mood—turn the lights down low, open every closet and overhead bin so there is *no* question where to stow your luggage, turn on the "medication music," and place a sweet flight attendant at the door to greet you.

As the passengers stampede down the jetbridge like the Charge of the Light Brigade, the boarding flight attendant, whose expression verifies her recent lobotomy, utters a pleasant, "Hello, may I help you?"

A 6-foot-5-inch gentleman enters the plane with a garment bag larger than a Winnebago and asks the petite 110-pound flight attendant, "Miss, can you help me?" Now what's wrong with this picture? All of our preparation has been shot to hell!

The next passenger unloads her donkey in the gate area and pushes past the door. She's dragging Bloomingdale's luggage department inventory behind her in search of the foot-wide assigned space that will be her "home away from home" for the next couple of hours (or days, depending on her luck).

If only you had checked your nine carry-on bags, you wouldn't look like the Hunchback of Nôtre Dame staggering down the narrow airplane aisle: Your humps wouldn't keep getting in the way, and dragging what used to feel like your right foot wouldn't be so tiring. We share your joy in finding the correct row and don't worry about the three hundred people you're holding up while you decide the right position for all your luggage. The other passengers won't mind if you take as much time stowing your luggage as you do rearranging your living room. It's okay.

Other passengers play "Dump a Bag," which turns into "Hide and Seek" for us. They just abandon the bag they have managed to squeeze through the boarding door, assuming one of us will take care of it. They're right. We definitely take *good* care of it! We hide it and they can rest assured they will have a hard time retrieving it at the end of the flight.

Marking your turf has made you a little warm. You want to hang your coat now, but you're penned in by the window, so you hand it to us. We don't really mind, but hanging jackets with warm, wet armpits and dandruff on the collar makes us realize how glamorous this job is *not*!

A man with the breath of a thousand llamas has just asked us for some mustard for the hot dog he brought on; a mother has handed us an open, warm, musky diaper that smells like very old dog food; and we enter the galley in time to surprise a passenger vigorously picking his nose. He mumbles something bizarre about it being a lost art, we agree with him, and he tries to swim back upstream to his seat.

Did you know that you are all affectionately known as "The Load"? The company doesn't like to hear it, but one of the sweetest phrases in flight attendantdom is, "The Load dropped off."

A passenger recently heard a flight-attendant co-worker of ours casually say that phrase. He asked her if she was referring to the previous month's mishap when a sizeable block of external, accumulated frozen toilet matter dislodged itself in flight and *knocked off* one of the engines. (It was later found somewhere outside Phoenix, Arizona.) "Oh, no, sir," she laughingly replied. "'The load dropped off' simply means that our final passenger count was less than we expected. If I had been talking about that other incident, I guess I would have just said that the shit hit the fan!"

In a word, boarding is utter chaos, but for some unknown reason, once the passengers are seated and snug, they're ready to enjoy the show. Sometimes they even see more than their ticket entitled them to . . .

It looks like everyone's finally situated. The drill is over. You get an A+. Let's see if we can do that in reverse. All strapped in and nowhere to go: YOUR FLIGHT IS CANCELED!

✈

A disgruntled passenger stood at the ticket counter arguing with the agent: "Ma'am, I would like you to take this suitcase, send it first to Chicago, then to Seattle, continuing to Los Angeles, and finally on to Dallas."

The agent replied disapprovingly, "Sir, I'm sorry, but we can't do that."

"Why not? The last time I flew, that's what you did to my luggage."

Touché.

✈

Before the flight began boarding, a gate agent was patiently explaining to a barefoot passenger that he must put on shoes or the airline would refuse to let him on the plane. The passenger told the agent that there was a terrific mess-up with his luggage from the connecting airline, and that the shoes he had been wearing had literally fallen apart. The agent felt very sorry for the man by then, and suggested that he try to buy some cheap sandals from an airport shop.

He obviously had no luck in finding them. We were hysterical as he shuffled on board wearing tote bags tied around each of his feet.

An agent had seen the chance reunion of two close friends at the gate area. They were taking the same flight and had requested seats together. The agent explained that the flight was full and that, once boarded, another passenger was sure to agree to swap seats so the friends could chat.

During boarding, the agent was called to assist the flight attendant with seat duplications caused by computer problems. To the surprise of the two friends, they had both been assigned the same seat. As the gate agent laughingly approached them, she said, "Well, when you said you wanted to sit together, I guess this wasn't exactly what you had in mind."

Boarding was especially hectic and noisy. And complicating the push and shove maneuvers in the entry area was the usual ace passenger who chose to live vicariously in the cockpit by planting himself in the doorway. He was observing the pilots as they went through their preflight checklists.

Desiring peace and quiet, the captain turned and, seeing the passenger standing there, said, "Oh, good morning. Would you do us a favor and close that door, please? Thanks."

Mesmerized by all the buttons and dials, the passenger had lost touch with reality. Closing the door behind him, he stepped into the cockpit.

"No, no, no," said the captain. "We need you on the *other* side of the door."

A Spanish-speaking woman boarded the plane with enough luggage to fill the entire first-class cabin. It took her ten minutes to store everything and get into her seat.

As the plane started to push back, the woman went berserk, screaming, "My baby, my baby!" The flight attendant, accustomed to working with eccentric passengers, started frantically searching overhead bins and empty seats for an infant.

Finally, a person was found who could translate. The woman did not misplace the baby on the plane. In all the confusion over her luggage, she had left the baby with the security guard.

A passenger walked on board and, in a voice that sounded more like a command than a request, said to flight attendant Lucy Hull, "Hang this, please."

Lucy was helping someone else at that moment and answered, "Just a minute, sir. I'll be right with you."

That wasn't good enough for him, so he decided to use Lucy as a coat rack and threw his coat right over her head. She just stood there and said nothing until the rest of us saw her and died laughing.

Rob has always been known for going out of his way to assist passengers. From a distance one day, he could see a female passenger struggling with an oversized garment bag.

He relieved her of the bag, explaining that he would hang it at the back of the plane. As he hurried through the cabin, the hook on the bag caught a woman's wig and jerked it right off.

Unaware of what happened, Rob continued to the back, smacking every passenger along the way with the woman's mop.

Passengers from the Caribbean islands always try and take on more carry-on baggage than normal travelers. Agents, as well as flight attendants, understand many of these people's poverty and try to accommodate all of their belongings in the cabin, helping them avoid extra checked-baggage charges.

Just when we think we've seen it all, someone surprises us. In the past month passengers have brought on a porcelain sink, a toilet, and a portable dishwasher. But this one takes the cake.

We were performing our preflight safety checks. Seated in the DC10 main cabin was a family of five with a car fender stretched across the entire row.

Anita was working in the back galley of a 727 and was frantically making preparations for a full passenger load. Five minutes before departure, she peeked out into the cabin and saw ten heads. Relieved that the passenger count had dropped off, she decided to find out from the head flight attendant what had happened.

As she passed through the aisles, she started giggling to herself. The plane was full . . . full of midgets on their way to a convention in Chicago.

Aliens

Uh, Denver center, this is Allegiance forty-one west-bound on J-sixty about fifty miles west of Denver, flight level three nine zero. Are you aware of any experimental craft in our area?"

"Allegiance forty-one, this is Denver center. Uh, that's a negative."

"Well, we're all watching something up here—can make out a circular outline for the object. Its flight path's really erratic—kind of a darting motion."

"Allegiance forty-one, we now have an unidentified blip on radar. Can you see any insignia?"

"Not yet. It's coming closer, but we can't see any identifying marks on it. God, it's fast! . . . It's right over us. The thing's hovering just above and ahead, and it's blinding us with bursts of what looks like, uh, blue lightning.

"We've lost all electricals. Standby . . . Standby . . . It's taken off like a bullet heading two six zero true—over."

"Allegiance forty-one, do you wish to report?"

Okay, we all saw this, right? And we're all convinced beyond a doubt that this could not possibly have been even an experimental craft, right? So, if we report we're agreed we'll have to report *something else,* right??

"Allegiance forty-one, DO YOU WISH TO REPORT?"

"Denver center, Allegiance forty-one, uh, that's a negative. We do NOT wish to report."

Why is it that sharing of these encounters occurs with the outside only during the initial stages, until the vehicles in question are positively identified as unidentified? . . . until the pilots are absolutely sure they've seen a spaceship with occupants who have never heard of Coca-Cola?

Because "Do you wish to report?" really means "Do you wish a new career as a used-car salesman?"

Here's an example of a cockpit crew conversation that won't take place every day:

"What was that?"

"What?"

"Didn't you see it?"

"See what?"

"I *almost* thought, for a *split second,* out of the *corner of my eye,* that I saw a large, round, silver object that I couldn't *immediately identify* moving in the sky *somewhere* over there."

"Oh, yeah? I missed it—but you should definitely report that to the chief pilot when we land."

"I will. I will . . ."

Yes, there are specific forms to fill out to report vital intelligence sightings.

C.R.A.P. I

(Crewmember Report of Alien Pranksters)

This form is to be completed by pilots of U.S. and Canadian scheduled air carriers, military aircraft, and civilian aircraft.

Reporting aircraft identification _____

Date and time of sighting (GMT) _____

Approximate latitude/longitude of object _____

Altitude of object _____ _____

Describe object(s) as to shape, color, size, unusual aerodynamic features, sound, number and formation _____

_____

_____

Describe course of object, exhaust trail, and object's flight path/maneuvers _____

_____

_____

Describe, if observed, lifeforms occupying unidentified object(s) and any attempts at communication by either party

_____

_____

There should be plenty of these forms to go around since no one's actually used one since August 3, 1959—the day they were printed.

Airlines have decreed that completion of C.R.A.P. I mandates completion of the accompanying form C.R.A.P. II (Crewmember Request for Attending Psychiatrists). It's that simple. Management knows that normal people do not see flying saucers or space creatures. End of subject. There's no room for discussion of any kind (except, of course, with your assigned shrink).

"Come on, though. Isn't it logical to assume that after thousands of flight hours some of you have seen something up there that was inexplicable, unidentified, puzzling . . . dare we say, of alien origin?"

No shit. But usually it's not external to our aircraft, has managed to purchase a ticket, and is hitching a ride with us.

Although after flying the line a while we'd even look at Charles Manson as just another mouth to feed, if we choose to step back and actually register what we're seeing, somewhat deviant lifeforms become readily apparent. We do this at our own risk, however, because we've learned from experience that the gray haze approach to the Passing Parade is far less emotionally taxing than the Technicolor involvement plan. Meaningful daily interaction with 700 people could arguably stand one in good stead to outplay Mother Teresa in various categories. This is not the Peace Corps.

There are some passengers who don't feel they've gotten their money's worth if they walk off of the airplane empty-handed. Transportation itself seems somehow intangible, so it becomes necessary to collect souvenirs enroute. The lavatory is an excellent rip-off target because (A) access is permitted, (B) lots of objects are removable, and (C) one can always use an extra roll of toilet tissue. And the paper Dixie cups are cute for making little doggie hats.

Eating every bite of your meal will make your dinner napkin more than adequate for cleaning the ceramic dishes before putting them in your purse. Don't forget to take the dessert plate. And the knife and fork, too. While you're at it, just put the plastic tray in a carryon bag. That way, we won't be suspicious during pickup when we spy a naked serving tray on your tray table. The last passenger that attempted this made the mistake of leaving her purse on the plane after her flight. Upon reclaiming, her face said it all as she opened the purse to find "YOU'RE WELCOME" scrawled on all of the plates.

Although the flight-attendant seatbelts and O_2 masks used for demonstration also often mysteriously disappear, the hands-down favorite seems to be the underseat life vests. Please think twice before taking these. No one will believe that you brought it from home when you're retrieving the thing inflight from your own hand luggage should that action become necessary (see Splash, page 67).

(Let us assure the rest of our kind readership that cabin service routinely verifies the presence of all life vests before each overwater flight. No, they don't crawl around beneath 350 seats to check. Instead, they use a five- by 10-inch mirror attached at an angle to a 3-foot-long pole—sort of a large version of what the dentist crams into your mouth. They also use it to look up flight attendants' skirts until we wise up and learn to stay well clear of the area until the guys have completed their duties.)

Occasionally there are passengers who we're onto from the beginning. One man boarded our airplane with a large, square, vinyl carry-on bag that had the following printed on the front:

```
┌─────────────────────┐
│  Leastearn Airlines  │
│      HEADSETS        │
└─────────────────────┘
```

We kept an eye on him.

And then there's the mother leaving the airplane during a January blizzard with a sleepy child in tow who looks like a navy blue mummy wrapped in four of our airline blankets. There walks our profit sharing.

However, there are those passengers whom we do take pity on because it's obvious they've survived some early trauma—like being raised by wolves, maybe. We can rarely identify them in advance unless they say something at the boarding door such as "Where is trough thirty-two, please—seats A and B?" They live to create garbage. At the end of the flight, their row looks like the Gulf Coast after Camille. We're talking about a study in consume and dispose—enough newspapers to start a bonfire, empty cups and ice all over the place, piles of pillows and blankets, plastic wrappers, Velveeta cheese slices stuck to the seats, and a big pile of Kitty Litter—no, that's crushed pecan sandies—on the floor.

After we land, the tireless cabin-service people will make the plane spotless before the next flight. That's sort of like rebuilding a posh resort in Bangladesh each spring.

Is she having a seizure??

Of course not, silly. You've seen her. She's just doing those inflight exercises she's read so much about. But she's nearly out of control. The beads of moisture on her face aren't perspiration. She's overdosed on Evian face spray. And even though her nose looks like it's been ravaged by a *major* mucous-producing virus, don't worry. She's only packed her nostrils with half a jar of Vaseline to moisturize her membranes. She *is* worried about the static that's making her hair stand up like it's on top of a Vandenburg generator—no magazine article has tackled that problem. We say,

1A. 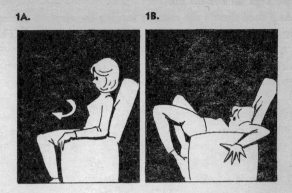 **1B.**

1A.  **1B.**

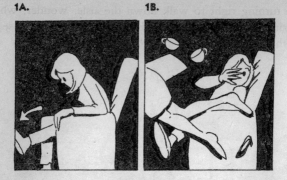

take out that Vaseline jar. She's determined to make it to her final destination looking none the worse for wear. Little does she know that she'll *still* look like she's been ejected at high speed from the spin cycle when she lands, but she's great fun to watch. We admire her tenacity.

There was the woman who wore knee socks on her arms throughout the flight. Yes, we know they kept her warm, but it was a little irregular. And then there was the passenger who managed to delay our flight for two hours while the bomb squad cautiously approached and removed her large piece of wildly vibrating checked luggage. The item they subsequently found was of a *highly personal* nature. And the night flight that was a bit strange because someone has scrawled the F _ _ _ word in 2-foot letters on the sidewall in that glows-only-in-the-dark paint. We discovered it as we turned down the cabin lights for the movie. Don't ask. We don't know.

Then there are the coach passengers who, accustomed to boarding the airplane through the lefthand side door and then turning right to walk down the aisle, wonder, when entering through the righthand side door, *why* we chose to put the First Class section in the *tail* of this airplane.

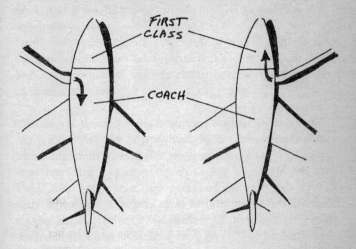

FIRST CLASS

COACH

We didn't. They'll catch on in a few minutes.

Even if what they're doing isn't offensive, it is at least *odd* to us, and it often makes us giggle.

In fairness, the majority of passengers treat us as well as we treat them. The proof is on us, and that's fine. It's our job, and we gladly undertake to do it as well as we can.

There are special people who will always remain in our hearts: those who refuse their onboard meal and feel compelled to explain to us that they ate beforehand either because they didn't know food was ever served on an airliner or that they didn't feel they could afford the additional expense, or those older folks who are often on their first flights and are counting pennies from their coin purses to pay you for their soft drinks or to give you a small fee for *your* services. Their quiet dignity is awe inspiring. It is a privilege and a pleasure to serve them.

The passengers we will always go out of our way to help are the "Oh-my-God-I-know-this-time-we're-going-to-crash" ones. They're sensitive, intelligent people whose vivid imaginations temporarily take over and who have confessed more mortal sins in airplane lavatories than all of us will ever do in any house of worship over the course of our lives.

They're easy to spot because their fingernails are embedded in the armrests, all of their muscles are clenched in tight little wads, their airvent is on full blast feeding their hair into the mouth of the passenger next to them, and even though they're trying to look bored, they squeal a lot. They look like the resulting mess of an imaginary nasty trick conducted by the head flight attendant in which the attendants are instructed to "Sit on your jumpseats and look terrified. It'll scare hell out of the passengers."

The best plan seems to be to get the panic-stricken person to focus completely on something that requires concentration. We'll get them started. This is a beginning worksheet for the next panic attack:

Add the columns of figures below vertically, then horizontally. Don't make a mistake!

189,845	790,380	897,597	357,379	=
793,680	379,379	579,564	785,683	=
689,767	789,467	354,678	784,834	=
886,795	678,479	379,574	378,756	=
975,678	573,453	478,479	586,875	=
867,457	489,444	657,449	985,637	=
578,389	478,386	579,389	478,999	=
968,378	768,978	996,856	567,479	=
687,999	787,823	236,368	781,462	=
357,647	678,345	648,379	279,576	=
578,379	982,389	372,333	450,374	=
399,677	658,679	983,233	470,168	=
487,398	765,556	576,692	998,928	=
973,329	172,448	852,339	328,974	=
126,379	111,379	986,797	329,925	=
997,960	941,994	489,279	332,668	=

Just remember, you're in good hands. Forward of the two front baptistries sits a god who's flanked by two archangels and who communicates frequently via radio with lesser gods flying in the vicinity. It's all set up like heaven. If you find yourself really losing it, grip your seatbelt buckle and sing this under your breath.

PLANE CHANT

Oh, please help this big fat airplane re - main a - loft, ac - cord - ing to_ its flight plan.

For mine eyes have seen the ages And my ears are sure that the en - gines sound_ fun - ny.
of the pilots,

O - pen thou my lips to show forth my craze. I henceforth promise to mend my ways.

Have mer - cy upon me, Have pit - y upon me, Have mer - cy upon me. Grant me some peace.

As I was in the beginning, nev - er will be, I'll nev - er sin . . . a - gain.
am not now, and probably

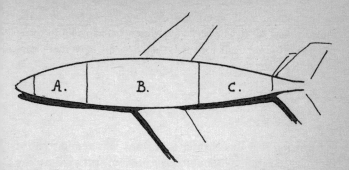

Actually, the plane comprises three zones defined by the various personality types that tend to gravitate toward them.

Zone A consists of First Class. People here are either working so hard or are so tired from working so hard that it's a very quiet area.

Zone B is only slightly livelier (the children are here) and is home to a vast amount of inflight knitting activity.

Zone C is basically a subversive outpost containing the smoking section and those undergoing aversion therapy; it is, in fact, very similar to the infamous *Star Wars'* canteen. The people seated in this section are rarely offered a choice of entrée—the logic behind this being that smokers have no taste buds to speak of, anyway.

It's by far the most colorful area on the airplane, where asocial individuals, paranoids, and people who are fine until their Thorazine wears off usually sit. It's smoky and hot, and you can eventually spot the guy who a few minutes ago was trying to drink through what looked like his ear, but is currently rocking in the corner telling himself that now is not the time to "fiend out."

You see, the smoking section is generally the area of

highest liquor consumption. And at 35,000 feet, liquor makes people, well, you know. We're glad we have had the opportunity to fly before all airlines ban smoking completely. No doubt our jobs will then become extremely boring and predictable . . .

GETTING EVEN

Knowing that this chapter is in some way reminiscent of the old "taxation without representation" tiff, we hereby provide for you, in the spirit of equal time, some highly effective recourse. Still . . . God save the Queen.

1. When it's time to initially board the airplane, under *no* circumstances have your ticket/boarding pass ready for the flight attendants at the terminal door. Take your time and DIG. *Slowly.* This will fluster the flight attendants because they've been conditioned to do everything quickly, and it has the added advantage of guaranteeing that other passengers will begin to push and shove, thus becoming an uncontrollable mob.

2. The boarding door has been closed and the safety demo announcement is well underway. When you're sure you have taxied out some distance from the terminal, tell the flight attendant that you have boarded the wrong airplane—you're supposed to be on a flight to Des Moines, not Detroit, for example! (We're in charge of verifying your boarding pass and we get in BIG TROUBLE for this.)

3. You have just ordered a beer that costs $2. Hand the flight attendant a $100 bill. (Note: This stunt may

backfire. Time permitting, you could get your $98 in quarters.)

4. The meal service is about to begin and the announcement is made: "Ladies and gentlemen, there will be heavy carts in the aisles. We ask that you please remain seated." Organize your section to go, one by one, to the potty. Instruct your friends that if they are hassled, they are to reply, "But I feel sick."

5. After the meal service, combine all five trays that were served to your family into one MONSTER TRAY and leave it in the aisle. It won't begin to fit back into the flight attendant's pick-up cart this way; but that's okay with us because coming down the aisle we can't see any floor-level obstructions due to the large cart so the tray will be knocked over (your cue to laugh). That's good though because it has to be disassembled first *anyway*.

6. The meal service is finished and all the disgusting trays of garbage have been picked up and stuffed into the carts. Tell the flight attendant that you have left your *passport* on your meal tray. (This is important, so we have to scavenge for this.)

7. During the movie, the passenger in seat A next to you has just asked for a drink. The flight attendant prepares it and, as she places it on the tray table of your seatmate, tell her you would like one of those, too. Continue this game through seats C, D, E, F, G, H, and J of the same row. This takes a bit of planning on your part, but the effect is well worth your initial effort.

8. Trusting your own good judgement, zero in on the most offensive, least desirable, generally disgusting passenger you can find (inebriated–yet–still–standing, odor–producing passengers are always good candidates). Tell him or her that you overheard *that* flight attendant (point him or her out) lusting after your selected candidate but vowing to play hard to get. Walk away and observe.

9. Tell the flight attendants you're an FAA Inspector but that you're not TECHNICALLY performing a checkride.

10. Laden with carry–on luggage, prepare to exit the aircraft. At the appropriate moment as you squeeze past the flight attendant at the door, JAB HARD. You can always say you tripped.

This is merely a partial how–to list. In this department, you are limited only by your imagination.

It really can be entertaining to watch a mild-mannered businessman turn into the Fernwood Flasher, but it's the little old lady that transforms into a rabid Spuds MacKenzie who concerns us (see stories that follow).

That's when management's rule, "The passenger is always right," works to our advantage. If you think you're a dog, so be it. We were told that if we played along, no one would ever get hurt.

We were also told that deregulation was an impossibility.

✈

Flight attendants feel very protective toward all handicapped travelers. We usually go out of our way to do anything we can to make their journey easier.

Our passenger information list for the flight one day specified that we would have a blind passenger traveling in seat 11J, a window seat directly behind the first bulkhead in the main cabin of our widebody jet.

The inflight meal service had just begun, and Jeannie Thomas was working with the meal/beverage cart in that section of the aircraft. She approached the blind passenger in 11J, requested his entrée preference (barbecued beef or chunky chicken), and proceeded to set up his tray table, put down his meal tray, and deliver his entrée. The passenger thanked her for her help, and Jeannie, following her correct training procedures, then explained the location of all food and utensil items on the tray.

"Sir, your beverage is at one o'clock, your utensils are at about three o'clock, the entrée is in the middle, your dessert is at ten o'clock, and your salad is at high noon. Enjoy your meal."

As she pushed her cart forward to serve the next row, it occurred to her that the barbecued beef is always rather like beef jerky, and wouldn't it be nice of her to offer to cut it up for him? He thought that was a wonderful idea, so she cut up the meat into nice bite-sized portions.

One row down, thirty more to go. After serving the next row their meals, Jeannie obtained the beverage preferences from the passengers in row 12—a Coke for the lady in 12H and a cup of hot tea for the man in 12J. Because we never know how strong you like your tea, it's standard practice to let you brew your own at your seat. Jeannie put the cup of hot water down on the tray table, and placed the tea bag, sugar, and creamer beside it. She then watched in horror as the passenger in 12J very shakily picked up the cup of hot water and sipped it. Then it dawned on her what had happened. She immediately moved back to seat 11J and said, "Look at me! You can see me, can't you?!"

"Of course I can see you. What do you think, I'm blind or something? But I'll tell you, I'll *never* fly another airline. This is absolutely the best service I have ever received!"

When we pick up meal trays, we stack them in horizontal rows of three in the meal carts. A cart holds thirty trays, so on a DC10 we end up with ten carts worth of dirty, sticky, slime-filled trays after the meal service.

Can you imagine having to dig through every cart searching for false teeth? We've done it. The experience that took the cake, however, was when we searched for a rhinestone-studded G-string. God only knows what it was doing on the meal tray in the first place.

Teeth, maybe, but a G-string?

Our first-time flyers should learn that they can't take every word the airline says literally. When we tell you to "check everything," we want you to keep your brain with you, at least.

We were flying from Chicago to Los Angeles, a very exciting trip for our first-timers because they get to see the cornfields of Kansas, the Grand Canyon, Las Vegas, and the sunny beaches of California on descent.

Brian was working in the main cabin and was doing a routine walk-through when an elderly woman stopped him.

"Steward, will we be over the Rockies soon?"

"Gosh, I don't know," he replied. "Let me call the captain and find out exactly where we are now."

As Brian started to walk away, the woman grabbed him. "Listen, while you're at it, if the Rockies are coming up," she said, "I want to take some pictures for my grandchildren, so would you ask him to slow down for me?"

No problem.

A recent flight from JFK to Los Angeles had become heavily overbooked in the main cabin because another carrier's scheduled flight had been canceled, but seats were still available in first class. At the last minute, the agents threw the remaining standbys on and instructed them to take the last seats up front. Among them was a passenger who was most decidedly not accustomed to some of the more refined ways of society. When a hot-towel was handed to him, he tried to eat it.

A passenger named Billy had amused us throughout the flight from Huntsville to Nashville with innocent stories of his "down home" friends and of the messes they had gotten themselves into. As the passengers deplaned, Billy stood in the airplane doorway pointing to the jetbridge and shaking his head in sheer disbelief.

"You know, Captain, I've flown near six times now and I jest cain't figure out how ya'll always manage to park this thang so close every single time."

$$\text{✈}$$

Along with its special television camera in the cockpit, which gives passengers a clear view of the take-off and landing from the cockpit's vantage point, Allegiance Airlines has rigged up a special audio channel. Passengers can use their headphones to hear all of the communication between the control tower personnel and the pilots.

After take-off, on a recent flight from Los Angeles to New York, a very concerned passenger was desperate to talk with us. He had tuned us out when we made our announcements and missed the part where we explained that the air traffic controllers refer to a widebody aircraft as "heavy" and that our flight number was "two."

"Miss, are we going to return immediately to Los Angeles?"

"Why, no, sir. Why on earth would we do that?"

"Because I've been listening over the headsets since take-off. The controllers keep saying, 'Allegiance too heavy' do this, do that. I just can't imagine that with all the safety-related problems lately they'd let us keep on flying around in this condition."

$$\text{✈}$$

It seems like the Dallas flights are always oversold in the main cabin, and it is up to the agents to pick which passengers they will upgrade to first class.

Phil was working the first-class cabin when a woman

with a beehive hairdo sauntered up. He was sure she had bats flying around in the belfry of her teased and lacquered coiffure. She learned makeup technique from a circus clown, and her clothes had stepped with her right off of the plains of west Texas.

She asked Phil for a glass of white wine, and her twang could have shattered the container. With his usual flair, Phil placed the glass down, presented the bottle, and explained that the selection was a Fumé Blanc.

She raised the glass to her lips and sipped it, then smiling approvingly, said, "Well, the wine is just great, and I really don't think it's too fumé."

We're so familiar with the airplanes we fly that when we work a trip, it's like having guests in our living room. It's easy to forget how strange and confusing a cabin interior can be to infrequent flyers.

The son of a tiny, elderly woman had purchased a first-class ticket for her return home so that she would get extra attention along with the most comfortable surroundings possible.

Shortly after take-off, while we were in a steep, climbing turn, JoAnn noticed that the flight-attendant call button was on over the woman's seat. Meanwhile, she was standing on tip-toe shouting at it.

"May I have a pillow and a blanket, please?"

JoAnn approached the woman, acknowledged her request while stifling a giggle, and told her she would be right back.

Never seeing the stewardess, who had approached from the coach cabin behind her, the lady shouted, "Thank you so much" into the call button.

The whole crew had a good laugh over that one, and we

were ready for almost anything from her. But she even out-did our expectations.

The airplane was a widebody—a Boeing 767—and a movie was scheduled for the flight. Cabin service had placed the usual complimentary headset remnants in all first-class seatback pockets before the passengers boarded.

JoAnn walked past the woman and, because of the unusual position of the cord, noticed that the headset part of the device was still in the pocket, but that the woman had stuck the prong end with the plug up her nose.

"Are you all right, ma'am?"

"Well, I was feeling very poorly—but now that I have my oxygen, I'm doing just fine."

And breathe normally . . .

✈

It was nearly the end of the seven-hour flight, and most of the passengers were watching the arrival video or listening to the stereo.

As Lynn walked through the cabin, a small woman who had been wearing an unplugged headset and gazing out the window for hours stopped her. Glancing at all the passengers around her, then placing her hands over the earphones, she asked, "Honey, before I get off, would you please tell me why we all have to wear these things?"

Just regulation procedure, ma'am!

✈

Although airlines finally allowed married flight attendants to work for them, there was a group of flight attendants fired back in the sixties for becoming mothers-to-be. For many years they fought battles in court and eventually won back their jobs.

Beverly was a returning mother and was very apprehensive about her first trip on a "Club Med" flight. Remembering the days of polished, refined passengers, she was disillusioned during the first hour of flight. Walking through the aisle with her coffee tray service, she was stopped by a male passenger.

"Hey toots, hit me with some more coffee."

Startled by his casualness, she asked if he wanted sugar. "Yeah, and I'll take some of that cream, too," he said, reaching over and squeezing her boob.

Mortified, she ran to the service center with tears in her eyes and told her fellow workers about the incident. "What happened to the days of people being polite? Look at the way these passengers are dressed. What's going on?"

Ann, a flight attendant for eight years, pulled her aside. "Honey, Walt Disney died and so did the glamour. Welcome back to flying."

✈

A passenger spilled *au jus* all over his pants and went to the lavatory to wash them off. When he got back to his first-class seat, he unzipped his pants, took them off, hung them from the overhead bin to dry, and sat through the rest of the flight wrapped, at our request, in an airline blanket.

✈

A handsome man was sitting with a little boy who was surrounded by all of his favorite toys from home. The flight attendant bent over, looked at the boy, and in a very friendly voice said, "I see you're flying with your monkey."

The man angrily turned to the flight attendant. "I'm his father, and how do you know what my nickname is?"

Must have pushed the wrong button.

During a lengthy air traffic control delay at New York's JFK International Airport, an irate passenger on board had given up hope of making an important business meeting when he landed. Getting the usual, "We can't possibly do that, sir," from the flight crew as he demanded to be taken back to the gate, he decided to give the airline a run for their money. He got up, marched to the air telephone, dialed 911, and began to scream, "Air police! Air police! I'm being held hostage on Allegiance Airlines' flight number three. Come and get me!"

The aircraft returned to the gate . . .

People have been known to go cuckoo onboard. This must have been a real case of ozone poisoning.

A man had been on an airplane for fifteen hours straight, traveling from Saudi Arabia to New York. He had six hours to go until his final destination, Los Angeles, and it must have been the idea of twenty-one hours inflight that did it.

Without warning, he flipped out and, by karate chop, broke down the dining-in-the-sky lounge table on the 747. Desperately, he tried to open one of the huge doors and get out. After a frantic flight attendant telephoned the cockpit, the engineer came running back to subdue the man, and, not anticipating the agitated state of the passenger, was knocked out cold. Eventually, two male passengers did manage to bring him under control with the aid of the co-pilot and a pair of handcuffs. The engineer was unceremoniously dragged to first class.

All in a day's work.

A passenger stopped a male flight attendant, rapped him on the arm, and said, "Hey, aren't you Fred Dole?" Fred, startled that the man had hit him, turned and hit him back. "Yeah, that's right."

The passenger went on hitting Fred's arm. "You were the flight attendant on my flight last month. Don't you remember?" Aggravated that this man kept hitting him, Fred hit back. With that, the man's arm fell from his shirt to the floor.

Fred hadn't known the arm was a prosthesis and he certainly didn't know what to say or do. Mortified, he wondered whether to put the arm in an overhead bin or under the seat, or to just run away.

Laughing, the passenger said, "Don't worry. I'd have to loosen it later anyway; my stump swells in flight." Then he casually picked up his arm and screwed it back in place.

A flight-attendant friend of ours tells of an afternoon she was flying into LAX. They were on final approach when a passenger pulled her over. "What do you see here?" he asked. She looked, but didn't believe it and marched to the cockpit.

"Well, fellows, there's no doubt we're in California. Take a look out the window here."

As they looked out, they saw some idiot flying in a lawn chair that was kept aloft (aloft all right—he was at 16,000 feet) by helium balloons. When the flight attendant left the cockpit, she said she hoped the crew would stop laughing long enough to land safely.

The nut case was on the news that night so we learned our friend wasn't crazy. But the guy sure was. He said he and some friends had put weather balloons on that chair but never thought it would fly quite so well.

Airline agents always jump back after opening the aircraft door of an all-nighter flight. At first we just thought that was procedure, but after inquiring, we found out it was because the plane smells so rancid. Maybe the agents should consider clothespins as part of *their* regulation equipment.

Most major carriers offer their employees extremely generous benefit packages, including comprehensive medical benefits. As these costs soar, the insurance companies, along with the airline, monitor in great detail the validity of the claims submitted. We bet they all did a double take on this one.

Just before closing the airplane door, an agent joked about a recently released mental patient we had boarded on our flight. During preflight cabin checks we did notice that this person was talking to herself nonstop, but so what? We could excuse that: It's pretty much how *we* are at the end of any given flight. Besides, she seemed to be enjoying her own company, which is more than you can say for lots of others with talkative seatmates.

Well into the flight, she seemed to see us for the first time. Our uniforms must have caused something in her to snap, because she started yelling and screaming, convinced that we were asylum custodians (a fairly accurate job description, come to think of it) who had come to take her away!

She went berserk, throwing pillows, blankets, and carry-on luggage contents all over the airplane. Two male passengers initially tried to restrain her: She responded by breaking one man's arm. As Cliff, our head flight attendant, tried to subdue her, she snarled and bit down hard, inflicting a deep wound on his shoulder. With passengers' help, the flight engineer finally put a stop to the fun and games by handcuffing this lunatic.

After we landed, the woman was taken off the plane in a straitjacket. Cliff was rushed off to the hospital and given a tetanus shot (and a Valium prescription). Two weeks later, however, he was called back to the hospital for some tests. Seems the woman who bit him had syphilis, and he now tested positive.

Can you imagine Cliff's difficulty in convincing the insurance company that his case of syphilis resulted from this inflight "injury on duty?" Poor Cliff! He must have submitted forty pages of explanatory inflight reports.

We bet he'll carry a muzzle from now on!

A male passenger was acting a bit peculiar from the moment he boarded the flight. Once seated, he dropped his tray table, started tapping, and began talking to himself. The flight attendants were working in the aisles when all of a sudden the passenger jumped from his seat and started kicking the cart and screaming "Fuck you!" He leaped over the seats and headed toward a male flight attendant, still swinging, screaming, and cursing.

Tim, a soft-spoken flight attendant, intervened. "Sir, you appear unhappy with our service. Maybe we ought to sit down over a cup of coffee and discuss it." Talk about being ineffective. We guess Tim never heard that you fight fire with fire. He was knocked down for the count.

> T'was a flight from the islands
> And all through the plane
> Not a creature was stirring—
> Except the insane.

People love to do impersonations on the airplane, but sometimes they get carried away.

On a flight from Jamaica to New York, a drugged-out male passenger transformed into a frog and leaped around the cabin, saying "rib-it, rib-it." Being an island woman herself, the head flight attendant knew how to cope. She sat on him the rest of the flight.

At the end of the narrowbody trip from San Juan to Haiti, the flight attendant standing at the boarding door was puzzled. It certainly didn't seem that all 130 passengers had filed past her, but the missing ones were nowhere to be found on the aircraft either.

The mystery was solved as she went to the back of the 727 to chat with her flight-attendant friend, who was just coming out of the lavatory after freshening up. They were both in time to see the last passenger walk out the back door onto the catering truck, hop down to the pavement, and run across the concrete ramp to the terminal. No doubt it was siesta time for the caterers.

A flight attendant was boarding the Haiti flight via the rampstand and noticed a little woman waddling across the airport concrete, up toward the plane. As the woman got closer, the flight attendant admired her nice, new clothes and clean, fresh appearance. Then she looked at her shoes and noticed that the woman had her pantyhose rolled around her ankles. She took the woman into the bathroom and showed her exactly how to wear the newly acquired clothing her stateside daughter had sent her.

Ah! The innocence of some passengers.

When smoke started to fill the DC10, a flight attendant ran to the back of the plane just in time to watch a Puerto Rican man kill a chicken he had brought on board. His friend across the aisle was preparing to cook the freshly murdered bird on a Habachi. Yes, these things really happen.

I'll Get You,
My Pretty—
and Your
Little Dog, Too!

Over the river and through the woods
To Grandmother's house we go!

Well, over the river maybe,
but we hope not through the woods. Tears
the wings off. At any rate, you have decided it's time to GO
AND VISIT SOMEONE.

Flying with children is not as expensive as you may
think. Airlines have lots of special children's fares, and kids
under two travel free. No, we don't ask to see a birth cer-
tificate as proof of age. The agents won't hassle you if you
fudge a little. If you check in with a mustached "lap child"
that has probably been on his first date, they may ask a few
questions. But if the child looks seven years old or less,

they'll take your word for it. After all, you're the one who's going to sit with Baby Huey on your lap all the way from New York to Los Angeles. It's your business.

Mom has somehow managed to make her way to the overcrowded gate check-in area where she's next in line to sling it out with the gate agent for her assigned seats. The infant in her backpack carrier has just locked on to a handful of hair from the passenger in line behind her, the toddler is licking up a blob of something on the floor, the five-year-old has wandered off to talk to a drug pusher who looks like a Nazi war criminal, and the seven-year-old has gone to the airport toilet alone. Dad's not traveling with them. He's either already at the destination or will be catching the next flight out (which leaves in ten minutes on another airline—he's no fool).

Mom looks like a papoosed Pied Piper as she leads her brood down the jetbridge. We do feel sorry for her. She staggers on board with her open purse, a garment bag, the collapsible stroller that won't collapse, a tote bag, a diaper bag, and a brightly colored toy bag. And if you think you had a hard time getting situated, you should see this:

Because they've (as usual) arrived at the last minute for the flight (had to go back home to get the Go-Bots), Mom, infant, toddler, preschooler, and Harold are not assigned seats together. Isn't that fun? Once everyone's situated within at least arm's reach, things calm down for a while. We can tell from the mother's expression that she wishes someone would put her out of her misery. We know she's fleetingly entertained a wish that it were humane and acceptable to sedate traveling kids the way you do animals. Then the worst thing you'd ever contend with would be some pretty heavy drool. No problem.

As you know, airlines always try to seat mothers with

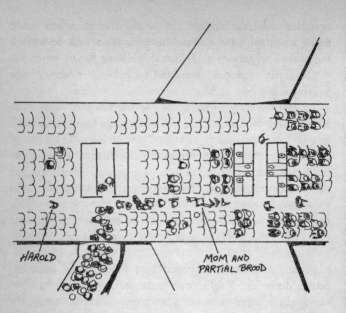

HAROLD

MOM AND
PARTIAL BROOD

"This way! This way!! THIS WAY, HAROLD!!!"

screaming babies in the middle of a group of working business travelers trying to make an annual report deadline—they are rarely seated with another mother because of those oxygen mask regulations (an aircraft manufacturer conspiracy; see Things That Go Bump in the Flight, page 182), and never beside a deaf person (the logical first choice).

It's time to play before the food is served. Playing with the tray table on the back of *your* seat is great fun. So is trying to get a small foot in the seatback pocket on the back of *your* seat. And there's always the open . . . shut . . . open . . . shutopenshutopenshut ashtray game.

Mom manages to dig out the toy bag, and the kids are

occupied until the end of the world comes, when some flight attendant fatso doo-doohead steps on and destroys a toy truck. Somehow it's less embarrassing for us when we trip over it and break an ankle (the kids get a bigger kick out of this, too).

It's time for lunch. Mom has ordered two special meals in advance—a hamburger and a hot dog. We have the meals, but catering forgot the ketchup and mustard. This is, of course, a major catastrophe akin to giving an adult caviar without toast points.

After two hours and fifteen minutes of playing with and throwing the food, the kids have to go to the bathroom, and the baby needs changing. The mother hands us a soggy diaper and asks if we have any extras. We give her what the airline keeps on board for these little emergencies, which resembles a personal hygiene device for a female elephant. After Mom straps it on with electrical tape borrowed from the flight engineer (it comes with no adhesive strips), the baby is abandoned to crawl around on the galley floor while Mom takes turns with the other children in the potty. Just finishing the meal service, we converge on the galley at breakneck speed pushing 250-pound carts ahead of us. The baby somehow survives this, and our attention is hastily re-directed to Harold, who is trying to open the door of our DC10, now flying at 37,000 feet.

After telling his mom that "this is the same airplane we were on last time, only we have different waitresses," Harold and the rest of the pack return to their seats (now buried beneath banana peels, Gummy Bears, hot dog remnants, crushed potato chips, Oreos, crayons, plastic kiddie wings, toys, and spit up). We radio ahead to alert cabin service that they'll need to change the seat cover when we land.

The kids discover the flight-attendant call button, and we are like Mexican jumping beans throughout the remainder of the flight. Mom (finally, thank God) threatens to break their arms.

Children traveling by themselves behave very differently. An "unaccompanied minor" is defined by the Rules Tariff as any child between the ages of five and eleven (inclusive) traveling alone. There are all sorts of procedures for keeping track of them: documentation that is given to the head flight attendant, introductions to the flight attendants working in the area where the child is seated, and mandatory ID verification of the person meeting or collecting the child upon flight termination.

We always try to treat the little passengers with special care because we know their parents have entrusted us with their most precious possession. Often the children will "help" us in the aisles during our inflight beverage and meal services. The children love acting all grown up; it's a great way for us to keep them in sight, and passengers adore it. Wouldn't your heart be stolen by a smiling, snaggle-toothed six-year-old serving you? (We're extremely careful about which beverages we let their little hands touch.)

These children are usually so well behaved that we regularly check on them just to be sure that all is A-OK. They'd probably be a little hesitant to approach us even if things weren't, so we take care to offer them food, beverages, and reserved potty space before conditions can become desperate.

Although unaccompanied children are welcome in the cabin, unaccompanied pets are not. Not too long ago, a woman secretly carried on two pet snakes in a cardboard box. The box stayed in the overhead bin throughout the uneventful flight. We took off again on the continuation of our flight following an extremely brief ground time. Once airborne, dispatch radioed us warning that we had the two snakes loose somewhere on the airplane—seems the woman had noticed that they were missing immediately after our departure.

Our all-female, nearly hysterical cabin crew found one of them during the flight curled up and snoozing in a stowage compartment over a warm oven. We never knew what became of his brother . . . but we keep that aircraft number filed for reference. I think we all considered turning in our wings that night.

We often hear our puppy-dog passengers howling in the pressurized cargo bin below when the tug pushes us back from the gate before we've started the engines. We always feel a little sorry for the animals: They must be concerned about what's happening to them. If we had our way, we'd turn the passenger cabin into Noah's Ark. Unfortunately, our airline (like all others) limits that kind of onboard travel to one animal per cabin (first class, business class, main cabin). Of course, that number doesn't include the animals that you can sneak on board. We won't say a word if your coat is wiggling around your middle or if we see an ear pop out of your purse. Be creative.

The only animals that we do have real objections to having loose on board are roaches, spiders, snakes, and rodents. You are usually not to blame when we find these. That's right, we do. Remember, these planes are like flying houses—there's even a special aircraft logbook entry for fumigation and infestation.

Not very long ago, on a flight from St. Thomas to New York, the cabin crew was forced to discontinue serving the meal midway through the service. As requested per the log-book, the aircraft had been fumigated several hours prior to departure, and the roaches were running for dear life—literally raining down on the passengers and their tray tables from the overhead bins.

Guess we forgot to include one item in our "Some Other Costs" table (page 85): Raid currently retails for $2.47; Roach Motel for $1.49 (plus, you can leave with a free in-flight souvenir).

Joy was about to pass through the security gate on her way to operations to sign in for a trip at JFK. A long line of people was behind her, so the security person was in a rush.

A family of six was in front of her, and after they put their eighteen bags on the belt mover, Mom and Dad walked through the checkpoint carrying toddlers on their hips. Their son, who was about ten years old, was holding a little doll dressed in a bonnet and one of those one-piece Dr. Denton baby sleepers.

As the security woman directed the little boy through, she grabbed the doll from his arms and threw it on the fast-moving conveyor belt. Suddenly she realized that the doll was a real baby, and freaked out. "God, it really looked like a doll!" the embarrassed woman insisted to everyone in sight.

When the security guard had realized she could do the baby more harm by pulling her out backwards, she let her go on through the machine. Mom and Dad were totally unfazed by the event, but Joy laughed about it the rest of the day.

Projecting from the top, center portion of the 727 cockpit instrument panel are three 1½- by 2-inch rectangular, red fire handles. These handles, labeled *1, 2, 3* in large white numbers, correspond to the left, center, and right engines, respectively. In the event of an engine fire, a loud warning bell sounds in the cockpit; and, after instrument readings confirm which engine is in trouble, the captain pulls the appropriate handle. This action shuts down transport of all flammable materials to and from the engine, additionally enabling a fire extinguisher contained in the engine to be discharged.

Upon boarding, the parents of Elliot, an adorable eight-year-old, had asked if he and a friend traveling with him could see the cockpit for a few minutes. We agreed and led two very excited little boys to the front of the airplane.

The cockpit crew gave them a very friendly greeting, and from the intelligent questions little Elliot was asking, it was obvious that the boy was extremely interested in aviation. Knowing what a thrill it would be for him, the captain stood up and invited Elliot to sit in the left seat of the Boeing 727. The child was in seventh heaven, sitting in the big jet with the uniformed cockpit crew. His shy friend remained in the cockpit doorway watching his every move.

"Elliot, do you know what we call that instrument with the airplane sitting on top of the line?" The captain was encouraging the boy to ask more questions.

"Uh-huh. That's the artificial horizon."

"Very good! Keep on going!" The crew was getting a big kick out of this little boy.

Elliot was on a roll and was determined to impress his friend. He turned to him and, with newly found cockiness, began pointing out and explaining the instruments and controls.

"This is the altimeter; here's how we know our airspeed; these are the throttles; this is where we lower the gear; here's where we set the flaps; and, uh, uh . . ." He hesitated as he pointed to the red fire handles. Thinking fast, he continued, "And we pull these knobs when we want to DROP THE BOMBS!!!"

We could hear the pilots roaring all the way in the back of the plane!

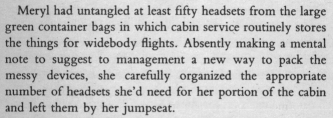

Meryl had untangled at least fifty headsets from the large green container bags in which cabin service routinely stores the things for widebody flights. Absently making a mental note to suggest to management a new way to pack the messy devices, she carefully organized the appropriate number of headsets she'd need for her portion of the cabin and left them by her jumpseat.

As she came back to retrieve her headsets for this New York to San Juan flight, she noticed that all but five were gone. She looked to the other side of the aircraft, where her co-worker was busily selling headsets in the aisle and couldn't understand what on earth had happened to hers. Perplexed, she searched the bag once again.

As she walked to the front of the aircraft, she couldn't believe her eyes. There was a twelve-year-old boy wheeling and dealing, hawking the headsets to the passengers for a dollar, and then pocketing the money!

What a deal! Why buy from us when you could get four for the price of one? We're sure that kid will be a great success on the streets of New York . . . selling watches.

After our meal service was completed, a mother with an infant took her place in the long line for the lavatory at the back end of the 727. Suspecting she only needed the lav facilities to change her baby's diapers, the flight attendant sitting on the aft double jumpseat generously offered to share it with the young woman and her child. She scooted over to allow the mother space to sit down. Noticing that it would be easier still if the mom had the entire length of the jumpseat to work on, the flight attendant stood up and began filling some beverage requests.

All was going well until the mother stood up to get some extra "wet wipes" from her diaper bag a few feet from the jumpseat. *Fopp!* The baby disappeared as the spring-loaded jumpseat retracted into the back interior door of the airplane. All we could see was a little hand hanging from behind the seat.

The mother stood there in horror, and before we could move to the jumpseat, our flying partner, Marcie (who was known for her rather sick sense of humor), said straight-faced to the mother as she pointed to the seat, "Did you know that everything that goes down there gets sucked out the back?!"

The woman fainted. The baby was fine. Marcie was fired.

✈

After landing, a flight attendant noticed that the Occupied sign on the lavatory door was illuminated. She opened the door to find a scared and shaking little boy sitting on the toilet. She started yelling at the child, telling him what a dangerous thing he had done by being there for landing, but the upset boy insisted on telling her his side so that blame could be place squarely where it belonged.

"That captain person told everyone to remain seated until landing. Here's where I was, so here's where I sat."

So there.

A flight attendant working in the lower galley of a DC10 bound for Dallas heard all of the puppy dogs barking in the adjoining pressurized cargo hold. She opened the compartment where the animals were kept, and seeing eight, furiously wagging tails, let all the doggies out and fed them the leftover meals.

She had definitely made eight new friends by the time the No Smoking sign was turned on for landing, and it was time to put the pups away. But, rut-roh, not one dog had a collar tag on. Little dog in little cage, big dog in big cage, and so on, was the best she could do!

It would have been bad enough if the dogs were all ending their travels in Dallas. But, unfortunately, six of the eight pet carriers were continuing through Dallas to other cities. God help the owners as they went to retrieve their dogs on arrival at the downline cities. We're sure some creative passenger service agent was busy explaining how altitude sometimes causes physical changes in certain breeds of dogs . . .

"Ladies and gentlemen, FAA regulations require that all your personal belongings be stowed either underneath the seat in front of you, or in an overhead bin."

After the safety demo, a flight attendant walking through the aisles noticed a woman sitting in her seat with a baby bottle in hand but with no baby. She tried talking to the woman in English, but there was a blank look on the woman's face. The flight attendant started rocking her arms back and forth with a questioning expression. The woman smiled understandingly, nodded "yes," and pointed to the overhead bin.

We were waiting in line for take-off sequencing at La-Guardia one afternoon. Everyone was eager to code yet another delay to air traffic control, but this delay was code-less—caused by an excited puppy that had found its way to the runway.

It took the airport and Port Authority police almost thirty minutes to round up the little fellow. When it was our turn to take off, the captain said over the PA, "Ladies, gentlemen, flight attendants: Dog gone; we go!"

A female passenger had repeatedly ignored our requests to keep her little doggie in the pet carrier at her seat. The dog was running all over the plane making a real pest of himself. When we had had enough of the mongrel, a funny, male flight attendant approached the woman.

"Madam, if you don't put that poodle back in its box, he might just accidentally get sucked right down the toilet."

Poochie went back in her case.

A boy, probably about ten years old, had been following Andrea around during the flight. His attentions flattered and amused her, so she carried on conversations with him as much as she could. Eventually, the demands of the service preoccupied her, and the boy felt he was being snubbed.

He could stand no more. He pulled her aside and said, "I

just can't understand you. I thought you liked me. You're just an enema to me!"

(Could he have meant *enigma*?)

Some behaviors are adopted early in life.

A dimpled seven-year-old girl dressed in ruffles, ribbons, and lace exited the lavatory closest to our service center area. As Tom, a crewmember, hoisted her to sit on a cabinet so that we could all gush over her, seventeen bars of our airline's minisoaps fell from between her legs to the floor.

Before our giggles began, she broke our astonished silence with, "I get dirty a lot."

Whining
and
Dining

Trans Global Airlines welcomes you aboard and is delighted you have chosen us to subject you to the finest in international inflight dining.

FIRST-CLASS MENU

– Appetizers –

CAVIAR

Gooey, glistening fish embryos gently ripped from the belly of the mother beluga sturgeon. Served with pancakes made out of buckwheat, but tasting like Spanky.

or

BARNYARD MEDLEY

Pair of blanched barnyard swallows smeared with a mustard paste and wrapped in the delicately salted and smoked meat from the back and sides of a pig.

— Soup —

CONSOMME "DEAD SEA"

Only slightly murky soup of warm water saturated with large amounts of salt specially imported from the Middle East.

— Salad —

HEART SAMPLER SALAD

The perfect marriage of cold, sliced hearts of palm, hearts of Bibb lettuce, hearts of artichokes, and hearts of dead chickens. Surrounded by a decorative ring of white feathers and served with a fig and egg sauce.

— Main Courses —

BUSH PIG "BAVARIA"

Filet of pork resting quietly amidst limp leaves of spinach, covered with a runny cream sauce.

CAPON CITRUS

Roast carcass of castrated canary rooster garnished with lemon rind.

RABBIT "RODEO"

Cold, barbecued bunny attractively arranged on top of Boston lettuce leaves accompanied by a fresh bunch of jumbo carrots (served with baking soda on the side).

STEAK "JOAN OF ARC"

Stump of dripping bull meat served with sunflower seeds.

– CHEESE BOARD –

An assortment of extremely old dairy products for you to sniff.

– Dessert –

CAKE "MARIE ANTOINETTE"

A two-layer cake consisting of a lower tier of vanilla shortcake separated by a chocolate crust from an upper portion of fresh strawberry topping. Both layers are encased in chocolate icing. (It is customary to separate the top half from the bottom, thereby enabling the flavors to blend.) A traditional French favorite.

AND FOR THE COACH CABIN . . .

SEAFOOD "GOODYEAR"

Stuffed blowfish garnished with prunes and served on a bed (pile) of wild rice.

or

"GET-A-LONG" CUTLET

A breaded cutlet of donkey accompanied by household potatoes.

All airlines try to hire a chief dietician who has been hospitalized or incarcerated at least once for aberrant behavior. That much is obvious to you. We'd like to educate you about what isn't, so come with us for a "backstage" look at what goes into your dining-in-the-sky experience. There's nothing to be afraid of . . . you're all grown up.

When they're not closed down due to FFDA violations, airline catering kitchens work like a giant assembly line. The prefilled, individual plastic salad and dessert containers are slapped onto the meal trays along with butter, rolls, utensils, napkins, and coffee cups. Thirty of them are then loaded into each of our airplane aisle serving carts. The entrées are portioned in the little ceramic dishes, covered with aluminum foil, and loaded into three removable wire racks at the top of each cart. They'll be reloaded into the ovens by the sweating galley flight attendant after they're wheeled over on the trucks, turned upside down, shaken up, and slammed into the galley by an outlaw band called "catering."

Yes, special meal orders are rumored to be available: low cholesterol, low sodium, diabetic, vegetarian, hamburgers, hot dogs, fried chicken, seafood platters, kosher, Catholic Catfish, Buddha Burgers, and so on. All of them are assembled in our catering kitchens, except the "religious" meals, which are obtained from a remote "blessing facility."

PLEASE NOTE: Due to the touchy political climate, publicly claiming a special meal could result in an international incident. STAY IN YOUR ORIGINALLY ASSIGNED SEATS. We can get you and your special meal order together via our paperwork. Do not make us cause you to call attention to yourself by having to announce: "Would Mr. O'Brien please identify himself to a flight attendant by ringing his call button. This is in reference to a KOSHER meal order."

Unless you placed your order in the previous decade, airlines will be hard pressed to admit you requested a special meal far enough in advance. You will find that the meal is nowhere, and we will find you screaming in our faces. Because most flight attendants are aware of this fact, when you come on board asking about your special meal order, we'll look at you like Jerry Falwell would look at an atheist.

On a narrowbody airplane, working in the galleys is pretty straightforward. On widebodies (DC10's, L1011's, 747's), it's a whole different story. The galleys of these airplanes are usually located beneath the main deck and are connected to it by little elevators, or "lifts." The flight attendant working the galley position stays downstairs throughout most of the flight. (She/he comes up to go to the bathroom if she/he is really desperate.) The position demands very little contact with the passengers, or the rest of the crew for that matter. Communication is made only with the flight attendant in charge, through a crew interphone.

It's a position that carries lots of responsibility, and many senior flight attendants who bid to work down there do it because they love it. Newer reserve attendants who are condemned to it by crew scheduling generally find that, initially at least, it's a solitary, hair-raising experience.

Every piece of moveable equipment we use during our beverage and meal services has first been boarded through cargo doors into our galleys downstairs. The galley flight attendant will send up at the *appropriate time,* in the *correct sequence,* with the *required contents* twenty 200-pound carts; enough ice for 600 drinks; 16 coffee pots; containers of wine, beer, milk, napkins, peanuts, swizzle sticks . . . the list seems endless—especially when you're new. Plus, there's the small task of actually cooking 320 meals, then distributing the entrée choices correctly and ensuring that the special meals get put into the cart that's located where you'll be sitting in the cabin. No, catering does none of this for us.

On the opposite page is a packing diagram of a "lower lobe" (downstairs) galley.

You are the new galley flight attendant, and I'm in charge of this flight. Ready? GO!

"OK, I want first-class predeparture, all coach liquor carts, both waste carts, the aft supply cart, my storage cart, coffee pots, four inserts of ice, a rack of wine glasses, hot towels and tongs, serving trays, all linens, napkins, creamers, sugars, two ice buckets, and the cockpit beverage container up before pushback. We have forty special meals today—here's the list. Of course, I'll want them placed in the appropriate meal carts for the main cabin. I *do* preposition meal carts 'aft-forward,' so be sure the meals are hot, hot, hot—about 165 degrees usually does it. Keeps the health department (health department?) off our backs! And

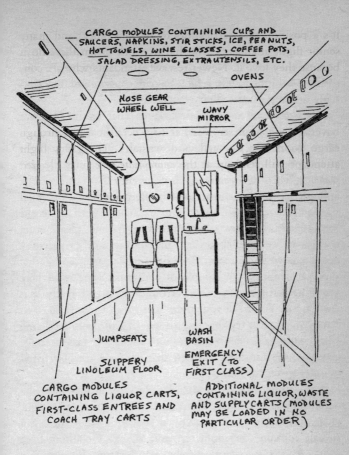

CARGO MODULES CONTAINING CUPS AND SAUCERS, NAPKINS, STIR STICKS, ICE, PEANUTS, HOT TOWELS, WINE GLASSES, COFFEE POTS, SALAD DRESSING, EXTRA UTENSILS, ETC.

OVENS

NOSE GEAR WHEEL WELL

WAVY MIRROR

JUMPSEATS

WASH BASIN

SLIPPERY LINOLEUM FLOOR

EMERGENCY EXIT (TO FIRST CLASS)

CARGO MODULES CONTAINING LIQUOR CARTS, FIRST-CLASS ENTREES AND COACH TRAY CARTS

ADDITIONAL MODULES CONTAINING LIQUOR, WASTE AND SUPPLY CARTS (MODULES MAY BE LOADED IN NO PARTICULAR ORDER)

if there's a partial, send that up first. Don't be late with the meals. I want them immediately after the cocktail service—I like to keep the service flowing. And, oh, . . ."

Got that, stupid? The new flight attendant is wondering if she's having a very blond day or if this is really mindblowing. Three hours of a "galley overview" in training just doesn't get it. She's got thirty-five minutes to do all of this AND count and oven-load the entrées: She'll spend the first twenty minutes looking for the coffee pots, and the next fifteen sitting on the floor crying . . .

No, the ovens are not microwave. That would interfere with the navigation systems, and we'd never find Chicago. They're convection ovens, and we cook our food *just* like you do at home (assuming you are fourteen years old and making TV dinners).

Working in the galley before the airplane levels off is an alpine event. You will wish you had shoes with tire-tread soles to grip that greasy linoleum floor. Airlines please note: During February carpet sales, indoor/outdoor carpet may be purchased for a mere $3.69 per square yard.

After sending up a couple of additional carts, you take your first free breath. The surroundings aren't really that unpleasant. You have your own little room to work in, two jumpseats (better try them out now—it's the only free time you'll have), a private wash basin to use before taste testing, and a wavy, fun-house mirror that lets you see how tired you are going to look.

The number one flight attendant has issued the alert: She needs all meals up in five minutes. DON'T WHINE and DON'T PANIC. In training, they equipped you with galley gloves, a special cooking thermometer, and an exact cooking-time chart. After the first two weeks, you lost the thermometer and the chart. You've been told that the more practical rule of thumb for any entrée is "blast at 275 for thirty-five minutes." You did, and now it's time to finger test. Insert right index finger into chicken entrée; lick; insert right index finger into beef entrée; lick; and so forth. Are they hot? Really hot? Is your finger good and red? Is it ON FIRE? Then, send 'em up!!

It's a dinner flight, and we've completed the initial cock-tail service. This handy chart will help you passengers gauge your flight attendant's approximate seniority. Watch her carefully.

HOW TO PICK UP AFTER THE BEVERAGE SERVICE

1st year: Pick up glasses on a linen–lined stainless serving tray.

2nd year: Pick up glasses on a stainless serving tray.

3rd year: Pick up glasses on a plastic serving tray.

4th year: Just march through with a brown garbage bag.

Now it's time to serve the meal. Here's how:

(DON'T BOTHER TO READ THIS)

(Suffice it to say that the meal service choreography, de-tailed on following page, is as confusing to a new flight attendant as a half-time marching band formation program is to a dyslexic.)

Put your wallets away. Your meal is included in the price of your ticket—well, sort of. Your ticket technically pro-vides you *only* with transportation to your destination: The meal is simply complimentary. Once again, you get what you pay for (nothing). Keeping this fact in mind will help to explain what follows.

The feeding frenzy in the cabin is about to begin. There have now been so many inquiries as to the start time of the event that we assume you all have been given a hot tip on a

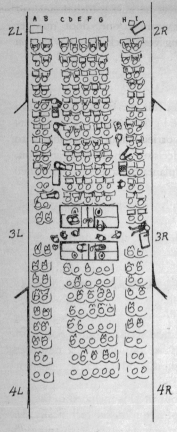

Phase I: F/A's I, E, J, F deliver meals from first set of carts. F/A's G, H follow with beverage carts. F/A's G, H pull beverage carts back to doors 2L/R. F/A's I, E, J, F pull empty meal carts to door 2L/R.

Phase II: F/A's I, E, J, F obtain 2nd set of meal carts. Pull to where you left off. Resume serving meals. F/A's G, H pull beverage cart to where you left off. Resume serving beverages. F/A's I, E, J, F pull 2nd set of empty carts to door 3L/R and park. F/A's H, G pull beverage carts to 3L/R and wait for F/A's I, E, J, F.

Phase III: F/A's I, E, J, F retrieve 3rd set of meal carts from service center area. Resume serving where you left off. F/A's G, H pull beverage carts in aisle behind meal carts; resume service. F/A's I, E, J, F park 3rd set of empty meal carts at doors 4L/R. F/A's G, H pull beverage carts back to door 3L/R. Wait for F/A's I, E, J, F.

Phase IV: F/A's I, E, J, F retrieve 4th set of meal carts, and so on . . .

Main Cabin Service Delivery Diagram

famine. We're about to give you a new definition of "meals on wheels." Your only job is to pretend that this is your last meal as you mull over the meal choices. (Don't worry if you don't get the one you want—it all tastes the same anyway.) Since the aluminum covers are hiding the entrées, we feel like Carol Merrill: door number one, door number two . . . You're nearly breaking your necks to see what *that* guy's food looks like.

If you *are* given an entrée choice, you can bet it'll be "chicken or beast." One flight attendant we know wore a special serving topper that said on the front: "If you can read this, think about it before I get to your row: CHICKEN or BEEF." If you're really worried about your ability to make this important entrée decision when the heat is on, just sit in the back of the airplane. Your only choice then will be to eat or not to eat. Guaranteed.

Sometimes when you get your food, you will find that it's unidentifiable. Just remember: "If it's brown, it's meat; if it's white, it's sweet; if it's green, it's something good to eat." (Exception: chocolate cake in the brown category.)

The beef will usually be either (a) burned beyond all recognition, or (b) still wiggling—ask us for a complimentary club. Here's a flight attendant tip for you happy homemakers: When beef looks really rare, you can coerce people into eating it by dunking it in a glass of very hot water for ten seconds. It's still rare, but no longer bloody (although it's a little *wet*). Chicken travels a bit better. It's genetic heritage enables it to remain more or less intact at high altitudes.

As the line of scrimmage moves aft down the aisle, the backfield is coping with beverage orders. Yes, everything (soft drinks, milk, coffee, tea, water, liquor, and wine) is available. It tickles us when you ask what vintage our Chardonnay in a Drum is. Forget it: The wine doubles as a disinfectant.

Catering, cooking, and serving fiascos do occur. Often.

We've poured port through pantyhose (clean pantyhose) because catering forgot the strainer; seen what we thought were pepper granules crawl around on your salads; witnessed ants marching across the chocolate icing tundra of your dessert (we're to save the bugs, if possible, for evidence later); and confused rolls containing ergot with caraway-seed bread. All of our apples look like they participated in that celebrated bout with original sin; the meat sometimes glows with a faint, purple color due to all of the preservatives pumped into it; and, yes, the abrasions in your mouth are probably from the mummified bread you just choked on. We only occasionally find glass in food—but don't worry: To our knowledge, it's been found only in cockpit crew(!) meals.

Only one tray set-up and entrée is catered per passenger (if we're lucky. Sometimes we're even shorted meals, and none of us can duplicate that trick with the fishes). If we drop a roll on the floor, guess what—it's going right back on the tray.

But the worst is when you ask for milk in your coffee, and we pour in what looks like cottage cheese from the milk carton. We stand in the aisle mortified and keep repeating to ourselves "Do not run away; it's not my fault, do not run away. . . ." Lots of times we'd be less embarrassed to just give you a Twinkie and a Coke.

Knowing all of these things presents us with a real moral dilemma. When we say "Want to eat?" and you say "Why not?" should we tell you?

It's time to pick up the mess. Our carts are empty now, so we can build up some speed pushing them around. How are points awarded for destroying body parts with the carts in the aisles?

1.0 point for shoulders

1.5 points for a hand and an arm

2.0 points for a leg (plus 1 bonus point if the cart is traveling aft)

4.0 points for a sleeping child's head.

Your abdomen is now distended, your spastic colon is more than aggravated, and you're convinced you have a fur ball stuck in your throat. You feel like we've done this to you and then abandoned you—we're nowhere to be found. But we'll be back . . . we're setting up for the next service: distribution of antitoxins.

It's now our turn to eat. Unless it's an international flight, the company caters meals only for the cockpit crew. Is there something left over? You can find us on the galley floor fighting and growling over scraps like a pack of wild dogs.

THE FOREIGN-OBJECT SONG

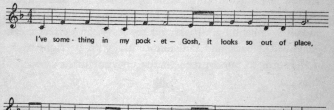

I've some-thing in my pock-et — Gosh, it looks so out of place,

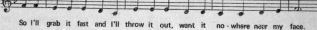

So I'll grab it fast and I'll throw it out, want it no-where near my face.

I know I'll nev - er guess it . . . if I guessed a long, long while.

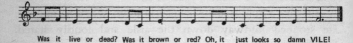

Was it live or dead? Was it brown or red? Oh, it just looks so damn VILE!

A SPECIAL MESSAGE

Mother Teresa, we hope you're having second thoughts about wanting to save and use airline food. You have such a wonderful reputation: Don't blow it. Save yourself, and the unsuspecting masses . . .

While plating our entrées for first class, we omitted the decorative sprig of parsley on one. As the young flight attendant was handing a passenger the less-than-perfect meal, she pulled it back and said innocently, "I'll be right back, sir. I forgot to put a green snatch on your plate."

We've given a dinner party for 320 people, so we're really tired now. There's so much stuff spilled on our toppers that we could make goulash if we ran water through them. If they gave us practical ones made out of Naugahyde, life would be simple: We could just hose down.

One of the dilemmas that we face as flight attendants is running out of meal choices for the passengers. It usually happens three-quarters of the way through service. Each flight attendant deals with it differently—some apologize, and others try to make a joke of it.

Biff gets a gold star for his psychology. When he ran out, he stopped midway down the aisle and loudly stated: "Ladies and gentlemen, may I have your attention, please. I ask you to all THINK FISH!"

We would like to know who in God's name dreams up the menus for our airplanes. It's obviously someone who doesn't fly and doesn't take into consideration all of the elements that work against us. Take our "Spaghetti-Sling" flight from Detroit to New York, for example. Have you ever tried to serve 130 people in fifty-five minutes with liquor first, then the spaghetti? By the time you land in New York, the entire aircraft, passengers, and flight attendants look like Three Mile Little Italy.

The flight that stands out in everyone's mind is the "Flying Flan Flight" from Jamaica to New York. In spite of the turbulence, the crew had decided to start serving dinner in order to finish in time to land at JFK. The tray that was being served consisted of cole slaw, fish in white sauce, and flan for dessert.

Wayne was scurrying up the aisles with a tray in each hand, and as he went to give one to a passenger, the plane hit an air pocket. The flan took its own course inflight and landed on the man's huge Afro.

Not realizing what had happened, the man tossed and

turned under his newly acquired bonnet. In a very discreet manner, Wayne tapped him on the shoulder. "Sir, let me get the dust off of your hair," he said, bringing the flan in for a safe landing by scooting it into a napkin.

We would love to have been flies on the wall when the man washed his hair that night. (Actually, if we were flies, we'd probably have been hanging out on his head by then.)

Lauren had had a bad day, and so had a first-class male passenger seated in 3E. As she came by to take orders for the inflight beverage service, she asked him what he would like to drink. "Hemlock," he said gruffly. He had already been very cranky and rude to her, and now he was wasting her time by being a real smartass.

"Fine. And sir, what will you have?" Lauren said, continuing to the next passenger.

"Oh, umm, Scotch and water, I think."

This one answered hurriedly because he could see that she meant business. She took the other orders for the cabin and never returned to obtain a more reasonable answer from the hemlock passenger.

After take-off, she was feeling guilty, so she decided to try to make him laugh. She served the Scotch and water, then served her special passenger a bubbling, smoking brew of dry ice in water.

He looked at it, looked at her, and exploded with laughter. Said she had saved the day . . . and he had saved hers!

One of our very close stewardess friends had just about enough of working the New York to Miami runs that we call the Kosher Klipper or the Bagel Bullet. Marge was summoned to the first-class cabin seat of a person who was obviously accustomed to the finer things of life.

"Miss, oh Miss, my potato is bad."

Marge picked up the offending baked potato and held it in the palm of her hand. "Bad potato, bad potato," she said, spanking it.

Because of the protection offered many employee groups within an airline by their unions, it often seems to the public that some employees get away with murder. It almost takes an act of God to make an improper conduct charge stick, leading to grounds for termination. We know of one flight attendant who has gotten away with just about everything in the book. We all love to fly trips with him because he does what the rest of us have always been too scared to do.

On this trip Jeff was working in the first-class lower galley of a Boeing 747. As we described, this is where we keep all of our supplies for the food and beverage services. The galleys are located downstairs and are connected to the main deck by little elevators.

Jeff was busily preparing food and setting up for the first-class service when he had a slight problem loading the rack of steaks into one of the ovens. Needing to inform the first-class flight attendant in the cabin, he grabbed the PA microphone and mistakenly punched the broadcast PA button instead of the crew call button. Over the entire airplane, for the ears of four hundred passengers, he announced, "Diane, first class is going to be a little late tonight. I just dropped all of the fucking first-class steaks on the floor."

Needless to say, the entire cabin loved it. When the food

was finally sent up and the first-class service was underway, an eighty-year-old woman was asked which entrée she preferred.

"You know, I think I'll have one of those fucking first-class steaks!" she answered with a wink.

It was a very turbulent flight—glasses flying, drinks spilling, and people getting sick everywhere. Yet the flight attendants kept serving meals to passengers who were mostly too scared to eat.

Debbie was trying so hard. She finished serving one row and as she approached the next with trays, she heard conversation from the first row.

"Did you see that stewardess' face? Did you see her look? I don't like it. I don't like it at all. That's the look of someone who has just served me my very last meal."

Definitely a paranoid bunch that day!

The Princess
and the Pee

1. Beneath the United States' most heavily trafficked commercial air routes, is it still necessary for farmers to fertilize their crops?

2. Has it been a very, very long time since you have heard or read reports of debris raining down on, say, Cincinnati, Ohio?

3. Would it be a BAD IDEA to have an open hole leading from inside a pressurized cubicle to the outdoors at an altitude of 35,000 feet?

If you have answered yes to all of the preceding questions and understand your logical thought processes behind those responses, then you can figure out the answer to the most frequently asked passenger question: "Can I go to the bathroom on the ground?"

After resisting the temptation to reply that to do so on the ramp concrete would most certainly result in arrest or, at the very least, a large fine, we respond to a question that must have meant, "May I use the aircraft bathroom while we're parked here at the gate?" (also read "without heaping grave embarrassment upon myself and my family?")

The answer is yes. This is not Amtrak. The lavatories have enclosed tanks under them. That's why after a five-hour flight with 320 people on board the lav smells like an outhouse at Woodstock. You can barely breathe in there. Airlines should look into a "pay-to-dispense" masked-oxygen machine in the lavatory as a new source of substantial additional inflight revenue.

There's not too much we can do about the odor while in flight, except maybe hang an aromatic coffee brew packet in there. Some poor ground-service person will routinely remove the external plug, connect a removal hose, turn a valve, and dump the stuff at the next stop. If you lose something down the toilet, *don't* reach for it. Wave good-bye. Jacques Cousteau would be interested in the entirely new life form (*Lavatorum vulgaris*) that we're sure has evolved down there 'ere lo these many years.

Your lavatory angst time is guaranteed to be twice as long as your ticket counter wait time was. It is also completed in phases. Phase I: waiting to decide whether you *have* to leave your window seat even though meal trays are still on all passenger tables. Phase II: waiting in the aisle behind the flight attendants still serving from the meal carts. Phase III: waiting for YOUR TURN behind the thirty passengers who have preceeded you in the line in the aisles behind the flight attendants still serving from the meal carts. Why are the other people taking such a long time in there? You'd never do that.

Because they're doing complete make-up jobs, giving themselves facials, doing their laundry, washing their hair, brushing their teeth, shaving, changing their clothes or their babies, writing The Great American Novel or reading the Official North American Airline Guide (see also our chapter entitled Airgasms, page 175). You will wish there were some sort of emergency catheter device installed at your seat. Or that you had brought a bedpan. May you use the first-class lavatory if you're a coach passenger? Only if visible signs of seepage can be verified by a flight attendant. A face contorted in pain just isn't good enough.

Leadership abilities count. Lots of valuable lavatory time has been needlessly lost in the past by people waiting for a lav that was empty all along. Don't be a sheep. Walk right up to that door and take a good, hard look at the sign to BE SURE. If it's empty, the little sign will say *Vacant* or *Toilet*. If it's occupied, it will say . . . *Occupied*—unless (these are tricky) a flight attendant has stowed her luggage in there, it's being used as a garbage bag holding pen, or it has been locked all along due to a mechanical malfunction (most likely).

Once you gain admittance, don't forget to lock the door. This is imperative since all airline lavatories are unisex. The expression "Don't get caught with your pants down" evolved from lavatory misadventures of hapless airline passengers. Even so, a locked door will not prevent the color draining from your face when you're sitting there doing serious business and some fool who can neither read nor understand the word *occupied* is pulling on the door handle so hard you just know he's going to come face to face with you at any moment. The survival instinct kicks in, and you're screaming "SOMEONE'S IN HERE!!" only 45,000 pounds of engine thrust is drowning you out. Bummer.

As pertains to all aspects of airline travel, before you get in, make sure you know how to get out. Bi-fold doors present a special challenge. And if you get stuck, we can't call the fire department. Read the signs.

There are three sacred rules governing the Airline Potty Kingdom:

1. Don't throw any foreign objects down the toilet (remember the "shit hit the fan" incident).

2. Don't smoke in there. It sets off the smoke alarm and sends us into an Official Emergency Mode. "Silver Mile-High Club" cardholders note: You will have to forego the ritual cigarette of satisfaction upon completing "you know what."

3. Thoroughly wipe down the basin for the next passenger. (There's a sign to help you remember to do that.)

You've been waiting so long by now that the No Smoking sign is on for landing. We're sorry, but you'll have to return to your seat. If you *do* manage to sneak past anyway, hold on tight. You're on your own. Landing in the lav has its rewards—especially with an inexperienced co-pilot at the controls. Bombs away.

But wait. The sign has just clicked to *Vacant*. It's YOUR TURN.

One word of advice: when it's YOUR TURN, attempt to open the lavatory door by clasping, then turning and pulling, the *round* object approximately opposite your navel. Do not attempt to clasp, turn and pull the clearly labeled item *Ashtray*. To do so will cause smoldering cigarette butts to ignite your shoes.

AIRPLANE LAVATORY DIAGRAM

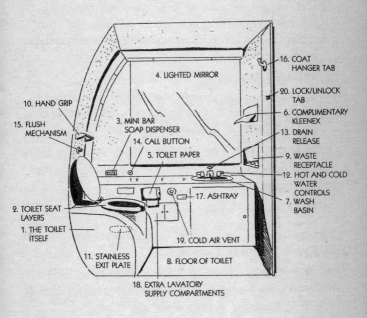

16. COAT HANGER TAB

20. LOCK/UNLOCK TAB

6. COMPLIMENTARY KLEENEX

13. DRAIN RELEASE

9. WASTE RECEPTACLE

12. HOT AND COLD WATER CONTROLS

7. WASH BASIN

4. LIGHTED MIRROR

10. HAND GRIP

15. FLUSH MECHANISM

3. MINI BAR SOAP DISPENSER

14. CALL BUTTON

5. TOILET PAPER

17. ASHTRAY

2. TOILET SEAT LAYERS

1. THE TOILET ITSELF

19. COLD AIR VENT

11. STAINLESS EXIT PLATE

8. FLOOR OF TOILET

18. EXTRA LAVATORY SUPPLY COMPARTMENTS

THE AIRPLANE LAVATORY

(Insights to a Fuller Experience)

1. The ultimate goal of your onboard pilgrimage.

2. Ladies: Due to the interminable wait, your mission will be one of great urgency. Exercise caution to predetermine (a) the cover lid is not in the down position, and (b) the cover lid and toilet seat are not both up.

3. Passengers have reported that the removal, counting, and re-insertion of airline mini soaps into the spring-loaded dispenser is a good way to occupy some spare inflight moments. Educate yourself as to the operation of this clever device.

4. Due to the slightly green glow emitted by the surrounding lights, the decision to delay no further your contemplated cosmetic surgery will be made in front of this piece of glass.

5. This material will either be nonexistent or will present itself in a tightly compressed roll impossible to unpeel by human means.

6. The entire box will be depleted by the first passenger to gain lavatory access.

7. Primary germ exchange area.

8. Must be maintained at a depth of no less than one inch of standing water. Also, designated area for disposal of used mini soaps, paper towels, and diapers.

9. A "dummy" opening or "faux-hole" that aircraft manufacturers decided to label just for the heck of it. See #8.

10. Provided to help you maintain a vertical position as you step on used soaps.

11. Stainless "flutter-plate" designed to admit waste items while providing the psychologically desirable illusion of a barrier between the passenger and the disgusting holding tank.

12. The more appropriate *cold/cold* or, alternately, *hot/hot* labels are unavailable. Spigot labels are sold only in sets of *hot/cold*—misleading as that may be.

13. Don't exert yourself. Congealed paper pulp and matted hair are difficult to overcome. Water overflows will be accommodated on the lavatory floor.

14. Basically, a superfluous item unless rung incessantly; however, is required by law.

15. Initiates automatic, inefficient flush cycle.

16. A retractable peg to hang garments on when you're in for an extended stay.

17. A prime example of lack of communication between airlines and aircraft manufacturers.

18. For your inflight entertainment. Something for you to snoop around in if you have failed to bring appropriate reading material in with you.

19. Gale-force device intended to alleviate nausea and sweats.

20. Correct use assures you some measure of privacy. Its importance to your mental well-being cannot be over-emphasized.

We have all learned the hard way that when people ask for directions on certain Caribbean trips, we must be very explicit in our answers.

✈

The DC10 has a little elevator that we ride to the main galley below when we need food-service items. The elevator door has a large glass porthole in the middle and opens up top into our service center area on the main deck. The flight attendants were milling around in there after one meal service when an older male "island" passenger approached us and said, "Baño? Baño?" It was a usual question, and we casually motioned in the direction of the nearest toilet.

Before we realized what was happening, the man opened the closest door in the area we had pointed to (which, unfortunately, was the elevator door), stepped in, unzipped his pants, and tinkled full force. Oops.

✈

As we finish our frantic cleanup during the last moments before landing, we dump all the leftover wines, carafe contents, and excessive liquids into the large first-class ice buckets, then hurl the whole mess down the toilets.

Jackie opened the door to a "vacant" lavatory and with flight-attendant automatic thrust, tossed the liquids toward the toilet. Alas, a passenger straddling the seat now sat drenched by three gallons of liquid. Ladies and gentlemen, please LOCK THOSE DOORS!

An enormous woman entered the lavatory and, because she had a fear of being trapped in there, didn't lock it—she decided to just hold on tightly to the doorknob. Another passenger, seeing the Vacant sign on, went to pull the door open. It only budged a little, so he thought it must be stuck and gave it a good, hard yank with both hands.

It was just like pulling a cork from a bottle. There she was, bare-assed in front of God and everyone!

A call light signaling for our immediate lavatory assistance went off in the flight attendant service area. The concerned stewardess rushed to the lavatory expecting some real trauma. She opened the door and the seated woman, with her pants on the floor around her ankles, calmly looked up and said, "Would you get me something to read, please?"

A new flight attendant with a charter airline had volunteered to work the Mecca run. She couldn't understand why there were so few volunteers for the trip. After all, the company would send you to Bali for a week of R and R after the trip was over.

Mecca trips consisted of Saudi Arabian people who had saved their entire lives to make this holy pilgrimage. They came from cities as well as from the most remote desert areas.

The new flight attendant's initiation to these flights began at boarding time. The passenger group brought everything with them: sheep, goats, tents, and wives. She knew she was in big trouble when a man came out of the bathroom and did a "butt walk" up the aisle. He didn't have a clue what the toilet paper was for.

She knew then how Noah must have felt.

✈

The Mecca charters are truly the most challenging ones for us. Many of the pilgrims have never flown on an airplane before (they have no idea what a meal tray is about), and have never even seen a bathroom.

On one particular trip, a male passenger had stayed in the lavatory so long that the flight attendants gathered outside to check on him. They were perplexed to hear the toilet flushing time after time for a good fifteen minutes and even more surprised by the sound of laughter emanating from the lav.

The mystery was solved shortly after the man exited with blue bowl water splashed all over his face and hair. He thought the toilet was a bathtub.

✈

The 747 was full; it was going to be a long flight. Spotting a vacant lavatory, Jan decided she'd better go while she had the chance. Finishing her business, she tried to exit. Oh, no. The inside door handle was missing. Fumbling with the opening, she managed to knock off the remainder of the knob mechanism, which fell on the floor outside. Ringing the lav call button for thirty minutes to no avail, she stayed there until the crew finally missed her when it was time for the meal service to begin.

The search party found her, but we had to get the flight engineer to let her out.

✈

After the main meal service was completed on the New York/Paris flight, Katherine lit up a cigarette in the aft galley—enjoying her first bit of relaxation since take-off three hours earlier.

On the pretense of having to use the toilet, the male passenger excused himself from his rather possessive wife of five years and made his way to the back of the plane. Introducing himself as "Jack," he engaged Katherine in casual conversation.

"Can you tell me what time we'll be landing?"

"Oh, at about 7:15 local time. Are you enjoying your flight, sir?" she responded dutifully.

"Well, the flight's okay, I guess. But I quit smoking yesterday at my wife's insistence—it's our anniversary—and I'm just about to go crazy right now!"

"Do you want one of my cigarettes?"

"May I—I'd be eternally grateful." His entire body relaxed as he took the first delicious drag and continued his little visit with Katherine. Before he returned to his seat, she gave him another cigarette to save for later "emergency" use during the flight.

Ten minutes before landing, while completing final cabin checks, she approached Jack's row. With a smile and a wink, she said to him, "So, have you done number two yet?"

The poor thing never got a chance to reply. His wife was already loudly accusing him of having participated in some kind of perverted activity throughout the flight that, from her vehement tone, we could only guess had been hashed out between them many times before. Sometimes it's best not knowing details.

Maybe their next anniversary vacation will be better.

Airgasms

You're bored. You've read the morning paper, completed the work for your meeting after you land; the music channel is broken, and you've seen the movie five times already. How are you going to entertain yourself? Be daring. Do something that only a small, elite group can boast of: Join the "Mile-High Club"!

Time is of the essence, so if you follow these five quick steps, your Silver Membership Card★ awaits you at the end of your trip.

1. *Case the joint*. Know where the flight attendants are situated. Your first priority is to avoid arousing their suspicions. You will always find two or three of them serving drinks and catching up on gossip in the back of the plane. NOTE: A good time for the caper is during the movie. Other passengers will be too engrossed to suspect the sordid activity that is about to take place.

2. *Choosing the victim*. Whether it be your traveling companion or the bombshell you met in the boarding lounge, make sure he or she is fully informed and get your watches synchronized!

3. *The distraction*. Both of you inch your way to the back of the aircraft. One of you enters the lavatory, but DOES NOT lock the door. (Beware: You may have unexpected visitors, so you will want to (a) keep your clothes on at this point, and (b) agree on a predetermined door-knock code. Your partner should attempt to engage in idle chitchat with the flight attendants, possibly even asking for a drink. This action will guarantee you an incognito status: You've made contact with them and thus are no longer of interest.

4. *Mission accomplished*. Ask the same flight attendant to watch your drinks while you go potty! (You had better pray during this time that your partner has been disinfecting the lavatory that has been used by 100 others in the course of the last few hours.) A few words of advice: If you have a tendency to be "vocal," the sound of the flushing toilet will drown out your voices. STAY CLEAR OF THE FLIGHT ATTENDANT CALL BUTTON!! A continual ringing will send the flight attendants running to find the source of the problem.

5. *The great escape.* Congratulations! You did it—but the escape is as important as the mission. Be clever! Do a final flush of the toilet as one of you slides out the door. Be prepared for a possible line of fifteen passengers who are waiting to use the lav. LOOK NONCHALANT. Quickly engage in a conversation with the flight attendants that have been babysitting your now watered-down drink. Don't be paranoid about the smirks on their faces—it may be simply because you have not zipped your fly. DON'T BE SLOPPY! LEAVE NOTHING TO CHANCE!

Just remember: THE LAVATORIES CAN BE OPENED FROM THE OUTSIDE AT ANY MOMENT. (But *that's* half the fun.) GOOD LUCK!!!

★ A Gold Membership Card for advanced onboard maneuvers is also available. The required activity must occur in the exposed airline cabin environment and must be dated, verified, and signed by a flight attendant. These forms may be obtained from any ticket counter. Enroll today!

One of the DC10 aft lavatories had the Occupied sign on for so long that we wondered if it had been locked by ground maintenance for mechanical failure.

When we unlocked it and checked, we discovered a neatly folded pile of men's clothing stacked on the toilet seat. Movement above our heads made us glance up, and we stared in disbelief. The ceiling panel, which extended across the four lavatories, had been pushed aside, and a man was perched on the upper ledge, sans clothing. He was providing his own inflight entertainment by peeking into the lavatories next to him.

Seems he took the entertainment problem into his own hands, so to speak.

✈

Karen Pawett was the sweetest flight crewmember that you'd ever want to work with. She came from a very small town and, even after eight years of flying, was still somewhat naive and innocent—perhaps a little less worldly than some of the other girls.

On this trip she was working first class on a Boeing 727-100. This plane is a pip-squeak version of the regular 727 and has one galley in the middle of coach, which services both first class and the main cabin.

Karen noticed from her preliminary passenger list that she was booked for four people in first class. Boarding was almost completed, and she took predeparture beverage orders. Only three passengers were on board, and she assumed the fourth would be a no-show.

She went back to the galley, prepared the cocktails, and walked up to first class to serve the drinks. Then she noticed that her fourth person had shown up after all. Beaming a big, welcoming smile, Karen greeted him. "Oh, you came!"

"I didn't know it showed," he said with a wink.

✈

A little boy of seven was making a real pain in the ass of himself as he sat with his prim and proper Connecticut mother in the back of the 727. She had warned him repeatedly to change his behavior. Finally, she had had enough. Making the most effective threat she could manage, she warned, "Okay, that's it. I'm going to tell Grandma never to buy you any more toys!"

The obnoxious brat refused to lose a good thing without a fight. He stuck out his tongue at his mother and in a voice loud enough for all in the area to hear, said, "If you tell Grandma not to buy me any more toys, I'm gonna tell her I saw you put Daddy's weenie in your mouth!"

We know, we know. But it's *true*.

Poor Joan learned the meaning of "clear air turbulence" the hard way. The aircraft had hit an air pocket and everything went flying. Trying to grab anything nearby and hold on tight, Joan groped for what she thought was an armrest. But when she heard a scream, she realized she had taken hold of the crotch of a male passenger.

Later, though, he did offer her his business card . . .

During a rather speedy taxi-in to the gate, Sabrina was standing behind the coat compartment by the forward door of a 727. She was out of sight of the passengers and a bit disheveled, so she raised her skirt to pull her blouse down. She got it waist high, when the captain made a sharp, left turn that threw her up against the lavatory across the cabin—in full view of the passengers.

The captain said all the good-byes on that trip. She was so embarrassed that she stayed in the bathroom as the passengers left the airplane.

But there also was a captain we knew who stood at the cockpit door, smiling and happily bidding all passengers a cheery farewell—with his fly completely open and partially hanging out of his pants. Not a single person said a thing.

A drunk and very voluptuous first-class passenger had stripped down to the waist. Although the male first-class passengers were delighted, the female passenger's actions met with no approval from the flight attendants. The senior flight attendant had tried everything, but was unable to get her to put her clothes back on, so the rather elderly flight engineer's help was enlisted.

He dealt with the situation in a creative and gentle way by explaining to the passenger that the female flight attendants weren't endowed the way she was, and that they were all feeling so inadequate that he doubted they would even be able to complete their service.

She never intended to hurt anyone's feelings, she said, so she got dressed!

What is it about the "Mile-High Club" that excites people? Is it the thrill, the chance of getting caught? We have all seen it at one point or another in our flying careers. Most of the time we ignore it, but occasionally we have a lot of fun with it.

We were flying that infamous flight #10—the 747 red-eye from Los Angeles to New York. Seated in first class was a top executive from one of the TV networks. He proceeded to get trashed, and the more he drank, the more he acted like an alley cat on the prowl. He hit on every female in first class. Unsuccessful in his hot pursuit, he went to the main cabin for a victim.

Victory! Jill and Peggy stood at the foot of the spiral staircase as the gentleman and his new friend started up to the lounge. After letting them get settled in they went to check. The man was "helping the woman put her makeup on" in the lavatory. Jill and Peggy rounded up the other flight attendants and waited for the couple to come out.

Fifteen minutes later the two appeared, and fourteen flight attendants were there to give their performance a standing ovation.

Heloise's Hints come in very handy on the plane. A young male passenger came up to the service center area where a group of flight attendants was gathered and turned around to expose the seat of his pants, which was covered with gum. He claimed he had a very important meeting in New York and that the suit was the only one he had brought. Before he continued, Janet took the matter in hand, told him to bend over, and with ice to freeze the gum, proceeded to pick the stuff off his pants.

As this ordeal was going on, another male passenger came into the center. Apparently loving what he was seeing, he said to Janet, "May I have a Coke, please? And while you're at it, when you're finished with him, I seemed to have spilled something here." He was pointing to the zipper of his pants.

We gave him the Barbie smile and sent him on his way, though we did entertain some thoughts of new uses for leftover ice.

Things That
Go Bump in
the Flight

This topic always stays close
to our hearts. The fact that things *do* go
"bump" occasionally is, of course, the main reason we're on
board. Your safety is of utmost importance to us. We've
been trained so thoroughly that emergency procedures are
second nature to us—but they're not to you, so we want to
introduce you to some basic ones.

One of our biggest complaints is that *no one* listens to or
watches the initial safety demonstration. This is usually a
cue for passengers to introduce themselves to their seat-

mates; mothers to threaten their kids to behave; and businessmen to bury themselves in the *Wall Street Journal*. Meanwhile, we're standing up there like bimbos pointing out exits to use in the event of an emergency and feeling like we may as well be reciting some unintelligible preflight Pledge of Allegiance.

Once we did a test to see if anybody out there was listening. "Pull the mask down firmly, and place it over your NAVEL . . ." The only person laughing was a five-year-old boy who was quickly hushed by his mom. She had obviously heard nothing out of the ordinary.

If only our safety announcements commanded the attention that the start of our meal service does. As soon as the first meal cart is rolled into the aisles, everyone drops whatever he or she is doing: Newspapers are thrown to the floor, crossword puzzles are put away, and necks are craned over the tops of the seats to get a sneak preview of what we're serving.

How about this: What if we hook rubber visual aids illustrating our entrée choice categories to our safety information cards? That way, during our demo we could kill two birds with one stone. You'd watch the demo to find out what's for dinner, and we wouldn't have to say "Chicken or beef?" three hundred times! What do you think?

> **"Flight attendants, please prepare for departure."**

Since the airplane is moving back from the gate, you reason, it has already *departed;* hence this directive seems to come a little late. What we mean to say is, "Flight atten-

dants, insert the steel rods that are connected to the emergency evacuation slides packed in the aircraft doors into the immovable brackets on the floor, so that just in case we all have to GET OUT REAL FAST we'll tear the slides out of the holding containers by shoving open the heavy aircraft doors, and pulling an inflation handle, will blow up long, fat, yellow things to help break our 30-foot drop to the tarmac." That's too long and scary, so we just shorten it.

"Arming" and "disarming" your assigned door is very serious business, and we have a system of onboard checks to make sure that each door is taken care of. Narrowbody airplane doors are armed by our squatting down and inserting the steel bar (girt bar) directly into the floor brackets. Widebody doors (which generally have larger, double-lane slides) are armed by maneuvering a lever.

The arm/disarm mechanism is conveniently located next to the door handle, thereby adding to the general confusion, so we need to know what we're doing before we touch either one. When you're new and a little unsure of yourself, taking care of "your" doors is like petting a pit viper. "Blowing" a slide on a widebody (especially inadvertantly) is an experience you will not soon forget. An exploding CO_2 cartridge will open the huge door faster than you can zip your pants. (In both cases you'll want to keep any body parts of value out of the way.) And the giant slide will inflate before you can scream "GET ME OUT OF HERE!" three times. Maybe four.

This kind of accident will, of course, cost the company THOUSANDS of dollars in delays and maintenance (slides are repacked and powdered more precisely than even parachutes), so your resulting confrontation with management is guaranteed to be a picnic.

> "As we prepare for take-off, fasten your seatbelt by inserting the metal fitting into the buckle. The belt may be adjusted by pulling on the loose end, and to unfasten simply lift up on the top portion."

Yes, we've learned through unfortunate experiences of trying to run to our jumpseats in the front of the plane just how difficult it is to move *forward* when the airplane is going 130 MPH on take-off. (Making your way to the back of the plane is no problem—just sit down in the aisle and your jumpseat will come to you.) The problem is that we may stop. And if we do, the value of your seatbelt will become evident.

There are important reasons why you need to know how to "adjust" your seatbelt.

1. It doesn't fit you. Either Dumbo or a munchkin sat here on the previous flight. Maybe you've gained a little more than you thought, and you can't . . . quite . . . *umph* . . . seem to . . . *umph* . . . adjust it . . . grunt . . . e-nough. . . . A new flight attendant will simply pound and stuff you into it, ignoring the fact that your eyelids can no longer close over your bulging eyeballs. A more senior flight attendant will be aware that the seatbelt she used during the demo is known as an "extension," and that it can be attached easily to the existing seatbelt to provide you with an additional segment of pure comfort. If you're lucky, she'll even have the tact not to loudly announce "Here's the SEATBELT EXTENSION you asked for."

2. You may experience A LITTLE CHOP (not a menu item— we're talking about turbulence here). A LITTLE CHOP may turn into A BIG CHOP or even A VERY BIG CHOP, and you'll adjust your seatbelt and sit there praying that the captain will just get the damn thing back ON THE ROAD. Severe turbulence almost always occurs during the meal service. We'll wish we were wearing sports bras, jockstraps, and suction shoes as we try to maintain a vertical position and reestablish contact with the floor.

French: Je vois les ailes qui bougent. Vont-elles tomber?
German: Ich sehe, daß sich die Tragflächen bewegen. Werden sie abfallen?
Italian: Vedo le ali muoversi. Cadranno?
Spanish: Veo que se mueven las alas. ¿Se van a caer?

English: I see the wings moving. Are they going to
fall off?

Non, nein, and no. They were designed to flap like
this (remember, we are *flying*); otherwise, they'd break
off.

Should you be frightened of turbulence? Yes, but not
because of the reasons you'd think. Turbulence causes
vomit volcanoes to randomly erupt throughout the
cabin. You never know when you're sitting in range of
one that could become active at any moment. Keep an
umbrella handy.

3. Did you see the cockpit crew come on board? Did they
all look twenty-six years old or younger? Then adjust
your seatbelt. Get the picture? If the captain looks like
the only adult in the cockpit, you'll still want to adjust it.
This could be the young co-pilot's FIRST TIME EVER to
actually land this airplane (it's expensive to do practice
runs in a DC10—that's what the simulator is *for*).
Remove your dentures and put on your neckbrace.

**"And now be sure that your seatbacks are straight up,
tray tables are stowed, and all carry-on items are either
beneath the seat in front of you or in an overhead
compartment."**

These things all must be done so that, if need be, you can
move unobstructed through the row, down the aisle, and
out the doors. Quickly.

> "Please read the safety briefing card showing the location and operation of all exits and additional safety features of this airplane. There are numerous clearly marked exit doors throughout this airplane, and window exits are located over the wings."

Please don't be embarrassed to pick up the briefing card and actually read it. We'll be impressed. In the wintertime, you probably won't finish reading it anyway because you'll be startled half out of your wits by what looks like pigeon blood being hurled at your window. Don't panic. It's only the cherry picker machine spraying deicing chemicals on the fuselage. Just be prepared enough not to scream when this occurs.

Now, back to business. About those "clearly marked exit doors." They're clearly marked if you're standing within approximately two feet of them. Otherwise, all you can see are seats, windows, and signs marked *EXIT* on the ceiling, and the ceiling is hard to open. Check out the printed diagram on the card, then look around the airplane and become familiar with your surroundings.

You may say, "This is all nonsense: useless knowledge I will never have to use . . . because if I have to get out fast following an emergency, I'm going out through the GAPING HOLE in the fuselage." But that's not necessarily the case. There is a good chance that you can get out safely, and there are evacuations that are required for reasons other than impact forces.

If you are to evacuate the aircraft (the crew will let you know), you must wait until the plane has come to a complete *stop*. Exit from a moving aircraft is hazardous, unless you're James Bond. You will then leave your Louis Vuitton and do as we say.

All aircraft exits are "plug-type" exits, and on narrow-body airplanes (single aisle) we'll rotate the door handle in the direction of the arrow, pull the forward edge of the door slightly IN first, and then open the door and latch it outside toward the cockpit. Period. Widebody doors are designed to open straight up—the door panels slide up into an opening in the ceiling.

Most airplane evacuation slides work automatically—when we open the door, they inflate. If they don't inflate, we'll pull the red manual inflation handle on the top of the slide.

Don't tell us that you'll go out if we'll get that big, yellow thing out of the way. It's there to *help* you even though it does seem to increase the distance to the ground. We remember going down the 747 slide in training from a doorsill that was so high that the slide looked like the "agony of defeat" ski jump. And they asked (no, told) us to sail down the thing by jumping into it from a standing position! (You must—sitting and scooting takes *too* much time.) They gave us painter's coveralls to wear during this exercise, and we wondered why until we slid down: It was sort of like sliding down a 40-foot cat tongue. Our backsides were hot from the friction. (Your pantyhose won't make it intact through this, ladies.)

We were all a little shaky initially to learn we would be working in an industry that acknowledged both "unplanned" and "planned" emergencies. As all emergencies were deemed undesirable, it seemed to us that, by definition, with a little cooperative effort we could surely eliminate the "planned" ones. Turns out it was simply the airlines' way of distinguishing those emergencies that come as a complete surprise (i.e., gear that collapses on landing) from those that give you some preparation time (i.e., gear that never comes down to begin with).

Airlines leave nothing to chance. We are given in-depth emergency checklists to use. The cockpit has these large, laminated sheets of directions, too. (They use theirs to eat off of.)

> "In the unlikely event of a sudden change in cabin pressure, the mask compartment located above your seat will open automatically. Extinguish all smoking materials at once, and pull the mask firmly toward you. This action starts the flow of oxygen. Cover your nose and mouth and breathe normally."

The mask compartment located above your seat will also open automatically during an especially hard landing. (Don't grab and pull. You can breathe on the ground—trust us.) How many masks did we drop? The more dangling masks, the more truly miserable the landing, the more likely the cockpit door will remain *closed* as you all leave the airplane. The pilots aren't fools.

If we do experience a rapid decompression, you'll know about it because you won't be able to breathe. It's like being in a giant Vac-u-form machine. Your "time of useful consciousness" with no oxygen up there will be only about fifteen to forty-five seconds, so you'll want to put on those masks at your earliest convenience. We'll be in the aisles helping you "don" your little yellow pig noses. Put out your cigarettes immediately. We'll be busy and won't have time to deal with the results of mixing pure oxygen and flame.

WHOSE MASK IS IT ANYWAY?

Here's something to keep in mind because you paid for it. In a rapid decompression, the captain will put the plane into a nosedive to get down to around 10,000 feet in about three minutes. Considering the fact that a normal commercial descent from 37,000 feet to landing takes about thirty minutes, you'll get some idea of what we mean by a rapid descent. The airplane's nose will be a lot lower than its tail, and all of the masks dangling from the ceiling will fall forward. You people in the last row of the airplane, grab those masks FAST. Otherwise, the folks in the row ahead of you will grab yours; you'll have none coming from behind you; it'll be just like musical chairs—"pop goes the weasel" and you're odd man out. Plan ahead.

Moms, please understand why it's sometimes necessary to reseat you before take-off even though you've settled in. Airplane rows have a fixed number of oxygen units and your baby in your lap sitting next to her baby in hers sitting next to the nice man at the window won't work. We're sorry that the agent didn't catch it beforehand, but we are always watching and counting. Thanks for being cooperative.

Yes, all of these safety issues (and many more) are thoroughly taught in flight-attendant training. We're even given an overview of the theory of flight just in case we ever find ourselves in Karen Black's position. May our hair stay in place just as hers did while we're flying in an open 747 cockpit at 550 MPH. (Our lips would be wrapped around our ears.)

Do we ever get scared? And do we really still smile when something is wrong? Sometimes, but you'll probably never know it; and yes, we smile in direct proportion to the severity of the problem. If we can't find change for the $100 bill you gave us for your $2 beer, our expression will seem to confirm your worst imagined fear. However, if the wing IS about to fall off . . . we'll probably look like Publisher's Clearinghouse Grand Prize Winners. Interpersonal relationships become very difficult for us—but that's another book.

The main idea is this: The level of training, skill, and dedication among flight professionals is extremely high. And although it's not perfect, we're here to tell you that THE SYSTEM WORKS. BEAUTIFULLY.

The next time you hear toward the end of your flight, "We should be on the ground shortly. . . ," don't panic because you *know* we'll somehow find ourselves "on the ground" eventually (the "what goes up must come down" argument), and you believe the flight attendant is avoiding telling you some awful truth. Reassure yourself that what we really mean is—WE WILL BE *LANDING* SOON.

Descent and final spastic approach into New York City had been so turbulent one winter night that we all expected to see King Kong eyeballing us through a passenger window. Since we had fed the passengers what only an airline could call food for dinner, it was no surprise that the cabin now looked and smelled like a messier scene from *The Exorcist*.

After great planning, LaGuardia Airport was constructed on piers in the middle of a foul-smelling body of water affectionately known to flight crews as "Egg Fart Bay." Pilots especially like the idea of putting major national airports in ponds. Since landing options, as you may imagine, are rather limited at LaGuardia, and since ditching is never desirable, especially in December, the object is to park the hurling metal tube solidly on the runway. The first time.

The captain tried to eliminate runway 22L with a denture-destroying, multiple-bounce landing that could best be described as a controlled crash. My jumpseat mate and I pulled our pantyhose up to the accompaniment of the number one flight attendant's welcome announcements, "On behalf of what's left of Allegiance Airlines, welcome to LaGuardia . . ."

But we were all safe and sound and at least one feisty elderly woman hadn't lost her sense of humor. As she exited the forward entry door and was bid farewell by the recently humbled cockpit crew, she stopped and said, "I just have one question: Did we land or were we SHOT DOWN?"

We had an oversold flight from Toronto to LaGuardia. Before we closed the door to push back, we did a seat count to see how many standbys we could accommodate. We checked the lavatories to be sure we didn't make a mistake. One of the signs read *Occupied,* but Joyce remembered locking it earlier when she stashed her flight bag there for easy access later. The other was empty, so we assumed we had made an accurate count.

Every seat was filled. During take-off, however, a person

opened that lavatory door and popped his head out. Joyce was sitting on the aft jumpseat, so she slammed the door on him and yelled, "Just sit down and hang on!"

We treated the lavatory passenger with kid gloves, offering our jumpseat to him while in flight, and then returning him to the lavatory for landing. We even gave him complimentary drinks in flight, including three bottles of champagne to take with him. Then we begged him to keep his mouth shut about the incident (the captain could have lost his license).

We later discovered what caused the fiasco. One of the other flight attendants had knocked on the door during the head count but had gotten no response, so she opened the door that Joyce locked. She saw the flight bag and hid it in a galley cubbyhole without telling Joyce. She had no idea a person was in there when she did her check.

All ended well, however. The passenger had a great story to tell his friends, and he never reported the incident to our powers that be.

You will probably remember this story—it was in the news a couple of years ago. After our FAA recurrent training procedures on the Boeing 767 one night, the mechanics incorrectly rearmed the window evacuation slides for the next day's flights. On final approach into New York's LaGuardia the next day, the airplane could hold its left slide inside no longer.

Bang! Kaboom! The flight attendant walking down the aisle doing a seatbelt check thought she saw a big yellow streak outside. But, no, that couldn't be possible. Could it?

After landing they all found out that it certainly was. The four- by twenty-foot slide had inflated outside the aircraft, was ripped off because of the plane's air speed, and found its new home in the unoccupied backyard of a Brooklyn woman.

A flight attendant was deadheading next to a woman who was an absolute basket case. The stewardess asked this woman why she was so nervous, and her seatmate said she had been a flight attendant with Divided Airlines. She had survived two separate plane crashes. She went on to say that the second "crash" was sort of amusing, though. When the plane finally stopped, the flight attendants started shouting their evacuation orders . . . except for one who went into shock. Instead of telling the passengers to "jump into the slide," she said, "Thank you for flying Divided. Please come again."

An exceptionally nervous passenger was seated close to the wing on the right-hand side of a 727, when he saw bursts of flames coming out of the wing. Not realizing that this process, called "torching," was fairly common to the auxiliary power unit located there, the passenger jumped up and pulled out the window exit. As far as he was concerned, the damn airplane was on fire. He decided to start an evacuation of the plane, which was now rolling at a healthy speed down the taxiway. Five or six people had slid off the back of the wing and hit the ground before we could tell the captain what was happening and he could stop the plane.

Have a nice hike back to the terminal, folks!

A family of four was traveling from San Juan to New York. The concerned husband had warned the flight attendants that his wife was petrified of flying. We had been walking on eggshells around her when we heard their teenage son go for broke.

"Mom, isn't this the same kind of plane that crashed a couple of months ago?" and "Mom, did you see that man out there playing with the engine before take-off?"

That child must have been dead meat when they arrived in New York.

We had hit some clear air turbulence that was classed as severe even for the flight crews. As Bonnie and Pat held onto the chair rungs after being thrown violently to the floor, Bonnie looked at Pat and asked, "Pat, do you think it's too late to call in scared?"

We vote for that special provision, too, Bonnie!

We had experienced massive engine failure (that means the engine blew up) in flight and were required to return to Orly Airport in Paris. After the initial damage assessment was made, we knew we weren't going anywhere. It was back to the hotel for another fun-filled night in Paris while the Parisian mechanics fixed the plane.

For the previous three months, Shelly had had the misfortune of experiencing mini-mechanical disasters in flight. At dinner that night, Bruce tried as only he could to soothe her nerves. "Relax Shelly, the fact that the chief engine mechanic used to work for Cuisinart is no cause for worry!"

In flight training we use the acronym KISS to help us remember the questions we need to ask the captain in an inflight emergency. This stands for *k*ind of emergency, *i*nitial signal for evacuation from the cockpit, *s*hould we plan to evacuate, and *s*pan of time remaining. One of our free-based flight attendants was obviously much confused about the use of this word. During an emergency, she walked up to the cockpit and yelled, "Kiss, kiss" to the frantic crew.

The cockpit crew turned around in disbelief. "You *are* kidding, aren't you?"

Lights on, but . . .

The
Grateful
Dead

So the flight wasn't all that you had hoped. This must surely be the ultimate protest.

Although we are trained in CPR and Red Cross first-aid procedures, we're unable to give the life-saving care that is occasionally required. The FAA now mandates that all carriers maintain an onboard medical kit, but the items contained may be administered only by designated health care professionals. And they're not always around when you need them.

When we're aware of a serious problem, we make an unscheduled landing at the nearest airport able to accommodate our type of airplane. The complicated part comes when you just slip away peacefully.

Being surrounded by blue skies, fluffy white clouds, and brilliant sunshine, and holding a double martini in your hand, is really not a bad way to go. Provided you have the proper credentials, at an altitude of 35,000 feet you probably even have a head start to wherever it is you're going.

If either your traveling companion or some other nice passenger brings to our attention the fact that you've been staring at the air vent for the past three hours, we'll initiate the appropriate medical procedures (hey, ya, ya, ya) and continue them until we've landed and help arrives. The rule is: We may *never* make the determination that you are gone.

In addition to the obvious ethical considerations of this directive, there are more practical ones. Besides the massive quantities of paperwork that would result from your onboard death, the coroner or similar official would most surely ground the airplane for at least a couple of hours. And we know what that means: downline delays.

Oh, no. You won't die on board, will you? After all the passengers have deplaned and you're still sleeping snugly against a window, we'll gently try to wake you. After eventually shaking you so hard your dentures fly out, we may suspect there's a "slight" problem. We notify the agent that met the flight. He'll call the airport paramedics to meet him in the gate area and will proceed (with a wheelchair if he can find one) on board the airplane.

We will then help him hurriedly collect the zombie. Abracadaver! You're alive again until we walk you off the airplane and into the terminal where you, at last, may be officially proclaimed . . . to no longer need your American Express card.

Rest in peace.

A brand-new flight-attendant crew had a passenger die on one of their flights. Try as they might, none could remember the correct procedures for dealing with death on board, so they decided to wash their hands of the situation and leave well enough alone.

They put a pillow behind the man's head, covered him with a blanket, walked off the airplane for their connecting flight, and left the corpse for the agent to find!

A man went into the lavatory at the beginning of a long flight from San Diego to New York. No one was traveling with him, so no one missed him when he didn't return to his seat. The flight attendants were so busy that they didn't notice his absence.

Just before landing, a flight attendant knocked on the door to get the passenger to vacate the occupied toilet. There was no answer, and she assumed a co-worker had locked-off the lavatory because of a maintenance problem.

On the ground the lavatory was routinely opened by cabin service, and the man's corpse was discovered. Yes, he'd been dead for hours, and by the time the authorities came to remove him, rigor mortis had set in. They had to take the lav door off to get him out!

A flight attendant noticed that a man traveling to New York from Chicago had a very large number of coach-to-first-class upgrade stickers in his briefcase. Knowing the usual allotment that frequent flyer passengers received, she was curious as to how he managed to have so many of these coupons.

He explained that on his last trip an elderly man had slept next to him during the entire flight. On landing, the "sleeping" man fell forward like a rag doll when the brakes caught hold. The airline felt so terrible that they sent him lots of stickers to make amends for his having to sit next to a corpse for the entire trip.

✈

At JFK, three Spanish men were walking arm in arm through the concourse to airport security. At the checkpoint, the security guard tried to explain to them that each had to walk through the door separately.

The men didn't understand a word of English, and they tried to push through together. The guard pulled one guy aside, throwing the other two off balance, and the one in the middle fell over like a two-by-four—he was dead, dead, dead.

✈

Michael Roberts is just one of the best. He tells this story from his first year of flying.

A woman with a beehive hairdo and a pronounced rural Texas drawl cautiously came aboard in San Diego for her trip to Dallas. It was obviously her first time on an airplane, and she seemed to be mentally weighing other options for getting home. She decided to stay and took her seat behind the bulkhead in the first row of the coach cabin. The meal service was underway when Michael asked the woman, "Would you like chicken or beef?"

Thinking the offer was much too elaborate she said, "Oh, no, I'll just have a grilled cheese."

"Ma'am, I'm sorry," Michael said, choosing his words carefully. "We only have those two choices. You see, we don't have a full kitchen up here."

She was terribly embarrassed, declined the meal, accepted a soft drink, and continued to stare out the window. Michael felt sorry for her and decided to try that PR stuff the airlines are so big on.

"So, are you from San Diego?"

"No, from outside Dallas. I was on vacation with my husband Harry. We own one of those RVs—you know."

"Oh, yes. So, is Harry driving the RV home?" Michael was very proud of himself. This conversation stuff wasn't so bad after all.

"No. Harry was backing up the RV, leaned out to have a look, and got his head knocked-off by a Mack truck. He's downstairs with us now."

Michael rarely starts a conversation with passengers anymore.

✈

Puerto Ricans have a custom for members of their families to be born and buried in the homeland. On more than one occasion, we have discovered dead relatives hanging in garment bags that passengers brought on board. It's much cheaper than paying additional flight charges, and, to be fair, the stiff condition of the corpse does help us keep those darn bags nice and straight in the closets.

✈

Catherine was working a junket from New York to Las Vegas. As she was tearing her hair out from the numerous requests for drinks, a passenger grabbed her and said, "I think there's a dead woman over here. Please hurry."

As she ran to assist, she spotted the woman—out cold—sprawled on the floor. Catherine bent down to check for breathing and muttered to herself, "Oh, God. Lady, please don't die. If you only knew how much paperwork I'd have to do, you wouldn't die on me now."

The woman's eyes flew open, and she started screaming, "How dare you! You've just poisoned me with that shit you fed me and you're worried about *paperwork*!!"

PART

III

GETTING
FIRED?

There was a little girl
Who had a little curl
Right in the middle of her forehead.

And when she was good
She was very, very good;
But when she was bad, she was horrid!

And when she was really bad . . .

We agree. There is *no* excuse, although there are
explanations. Yes, airlines go to a great deal of trouble
screening out individuals who just don't have the right
temperament for the job. But every now and then a few get
through who either can't seem to keep their mouths *shut,* or
transgress the rules in other, even more spectacular, ways.

The passenger is RIGHT. Period. That always has been and
will be the airlines' official stand regarding our on-duty
behavior toward you. They don't guarantee us that
passengers will always be nice or even reasonable; they do
demand our consistent professionalism and self-control. But
sometimes our most basic instincts get the best of us.

Airlines take a notoriously dim view of inflight antics. At
times these situations involve flight attendants whose years
of accumulated aggravation make it impossible for them to
still respond pleasantly. But there are other sorts: fun-loving
crew members who call it as they see it, crew members in a
devilish mood encouraged by colleagues they love, and

testy flight attendants who just have had enough for one day. One more run-through of the same tiresome explanation when you're doing a hundred things at once seems impossible:

"Sir, would you please take your seat."

"Why?"

"Because we're ready to leave now."

"So?"

"Sir, the captain can't move this aircraft until all passengers are seated."

"And why is that?"

"Because he has to see to back up, idiot! Now, SIT DOWN!!"

Since you expect, and usually receive, polite if somewhat reserved treatment from the flight crews, it's a shock when we give free rein to our onboard emotions. Somehow, incidents seem more outrageous to you than us simply because of our awareness of management's exceptionally high expectations. The forbidden nature of these actions contributes to their impact. ("Umm, nice. Who does your rag?" is not a friendly thing to say to a female Russian immigrant sporting a babushka.)

Think back for a moment to your days in grammar school. Do you remember the class clown? Who knows, it might have been you. He would instigate some disruption, and as soon as the teacher would turn back around, the little hellion would be sitting there like an angel with a halo around his head. The teacher wanted to shoot him, but his wit and charm usually saved his butt. Children like that don't change as they grow older; they just have to choose the right niche for themselves in life: con artist, actor, or flight attendant.

The next time you're on a flight and you see a crew that is

unusually giddy, you can rest assured that one of these hell-raising flight attendants is on board. We're never quite sure who the next victim of this prankster is going to be: a fellow flight attendant, a pilot, or even *you*! We cherish working with these flight attendants because we know there will never be a dull moment and there will be lots of laughs.

Their wings may be a tad bit tarnished, and the company would not consider them to be the quintessential professional, but for every fast comment out of their mouths, there's an opposing and endearing action. They are quick to aid an elderly passenger, eager to entertain your children with games, and, when it comes to an emergency situation, their performance is top drawer. They are kids at heart and are often misunderstood. We'll let you be the judge of that though . . .

The following stories illustrate what not to do unless you are looking to change jobs. And companies. And possibly your name. Owing to intervention by friends on their behalf, some of the "guilty" participants were only suspended for their infractions. The incidents were grounds for termination. Although not all resulted in that, some *did*.

Get your whips out!

Say What?

Ted was famous, and his fame just kept growing. He was working one of the first-class service positions on a trip not long after one of his previous fiascoes.

After the first-class passengers boarded, he was busy stowing luggage, offering pillows and blankets, and generally getting everyone situated. Right before the boarding door was closed, one last first-class passenger came aboard with about nine pieces of bulging carry-on luggage.

"Hang my garment bag for me," the man commanded Ted, who was frantically trying to stash the other eight items in all the secret jamming places flight attendants save for such last-minute emergencies.

"Sir, I'm very sorry but the coat compartment is filled."

"You must not have heard me. I said, hang my garment bag!"

"Sir, I'm very sorry, but the hanging bag closet is completely filled."

Knowing that his frequent-flyer status entitled him to some extra consideration, the man asked Ted, "Do you know who I am?"

Ted walked to the front of the first-class cabin, elevated himself on a center seat, pointed to the man, and announced, "Excuse me, please, ladies and gentlemen: Does anyone here know *who* this man is? He seems to have forgotten."

John Silver was working on the beverage cart in the aisle with a new flight attendant, Dawn, who had obviously never had a lesson in Spanish. On this San Juan trip, the two of them were to work with another flight attendant named Jesús Hernández.

Dawn had run out of Coke on her side of the cart and John had none left either, so she said to him, "John, ask 'Gee-sus' for some Coke, please."

John fell to his knees in the middle of the aisle and, looking heavenwards with outstretched arms, pleaded, "Jesus, send us some Coke." He was suspended for a week.

It was a night flight and a business executive had a huge pile of paperwork he needed to sort through stacked on his tray. He was going to have a hard time. His reading light was so dim that it was of little use, and no other seats were available.

"Steward, look how dim my light is." Comparing his light to the passenger's next to him, he continued. "His light is much brighter than mine. Now what are we going to do about this?"

Knowing the bulb could not be replaced in flight, the flight attendant replied, "Maybe you can get him to read to you."

✈

We were all bored on a recent all-night flight from Los Angeles to New York. Jim, a flight attendant who moonlighted as a hairdresser, was sitting in the service center French braiding another flight attendant's hair.

A female passenger who looked like 'who did it and ran' came in and said, "Oh, could you do me just like her next?"

Jim looked down at his comb, looked up at the woman, and said, "Lady, this is a comb, not a wand."

✈

A flight attendant was going down the aisles passing out magazines, when a smartass passenger looked at the selection with a smirk and asked, "Do you have *Playboy* or *Penthouse*?" The flight attendant said she would check for him and came back with a magazine in her hand. Leaning down, she said, "Sir, I think you will find the beaver shot in the centerfold to be most enjoyable," and handed him a copy of *Outdoor Life*.

✈

A passenger had seen Joe several times on the New York to Los Angeles flights. Obviously not understanding the program, she verified our initial estimate of her I.Q.

"Do you fly primarily east to west, Joe?"

(Now think about this.) "Oh, yes. That's why so many of these girls have wheels on their luggage. It's such a bitch walking back."

From the look on her face, she was probably wondering just how long that walk back took.

✈

A partially (no, completely) crazy captain stood in the cockpit doorway bidding every passenger farewell. Not one passenger noticed that instead of saying, "Thank you very much," he was saying, "Fuck you very much."

✈

An Oriental woman came to the back of the aircraft, where a group of flight attendants was engrossed in conversation. Looking frazzled, she questioned in broken English, "westwoom?"

Realizing her dilemma, but being a bit of a smartass, one flight attendant pointed to the left, then to the right, and said, "Westwoom, eastwoom!"

✈

Billy Bob Digger was one of the most vulgar captains around. He couldn't utter a sentence without adding at least one four-letter word for emphasis. His cockpit associates had long since become accustomed to his manner of speaking. One day though, Billy Bob went too far.

On approach to New York's LaGuardia, he decided to

make a passenger PA informing the folks that the day was an especially clear one. He finished with, "Why, you on the right-hand side of this airplane can see all the fuck the way to Montauk!"

He clicked off and with an "Oh, no!" look, said to his co-pilot, "Did I just say what I think I said?"

Yep. Sure did.

✈

After experiencing severe turbulence, a captain found a hole in the clouds and decided to make a steep descent. (We call it a slam dunk.)

The cabin crew was a very junior bunch, and the flight attendant in charge had been flying only one month. Totally flustered by the captain's request to immediately inform the passengers of the aircraft's upcoming maneuvers, she picked up the PA and announced, "Ladies and gentlemen, hold on to your drinks and nuts. We're going in fast."

✈

Her name was Clover, and, although she didn't waste smiles, she was more than pleasant—once you got to know her. She was a more mature flight attendant, met all troubles with a calm acceptance, and had a wickedly dry sense of humor—sometimes so dry that the passengers failed to notice it altogether. But she was a good soul.

A passenger had had a bad day in New York City. Delayed by massive traffic jams to the airport, detained by airport security doing random body searches of passengers, and denied (via airline computer error) his usual first-class window seat on the San Juan–bound DC10, the frequent flyer was destined to give someone a run for her money. And the lucky winner was Clover.

She couldn't seem to do a thing to please him, and, having run herself ragged for three hours, was pulled aside to suffer the indignity of having the passenger demand that she preview the bad letter he'd be sending to the company regarding her inflight service.

"Here, Ms. Clover. I think it's only fair that you read this letter before it goes to your corporate headquarters. Feel free to comment on it." Enraged and frustrated, he was shaking as he handed it to her. We thought he was going to explode.

Clover calmly took the letter, put on her reading glasses (they were hanging from a cord around her neck), knelt down by the man's seat, and slowly began to read.

"OK, you need a colon after the salutation. This should be a comma, this, a semi-colon, and this, a period. You need to indent right here, and your margins are a *mess*."

The man's mouth was falling open at this point.

"And what is this? Let's be accurate in our reporting: 'And then the flight attendant called me a Spic.' Now, sir, I've been working these Spanish flights for years. I would never call you a Spic.

"I called you a PRICK!

"Let me make you a drink. We can chat, and you can just relax."

His initial astonishment was followed by amusement and an admiration for her self-control and great sense of humor. The letter was torn up, and no mention of it was ever made again. They both still enjoy bumping into each other on the occasional flight.

✈

A flight attendant asked politely if a passenger would like some more coffee. He rudely ignored her question and simply thrust out his coffee cup so that she could pour it for him.

Duly offended, she remarked coolly, "I know where to put it. I just want to know if you want some."

Tit for tat.

✈

A passenger sat in the back of the aircraft drinking a beer and smoking cigarettes. Everyone around him was fast asleep, so he took carte blanche with natural bodily functions and sat there belching away.

The flight attendant sitting nearby was thoroughly disgusted with him. He let out a long, bellowing burp, and she tapped him on the shoulder and said, "Good tone, sir. Keep it up."

✈

A flight attendant who was none too fond of Dallas/Ft. Worth was working a trip from LaGuardia to Dallas. During boarding, a passenger glanced at his watch and asked, "Is Dallas an hour behind New York?"

"No, sir, Dallas is fucking *years* behind New York."

That one was worth a three-day suspension.

✈

We were ready to dish up and serve first-class entrées when a male flight attendant got on the crew interphone to enlist the help of a major queen working downstairs in the galley. In a sing-song, prissy voice, he broadcast to the entire plane:

"Oh, Brett, put on your pumps, darling, and come up and help me plate this shit."

We told the passengers that we must have received some strange radio broadcast interference over our PA. Oops.

✈

After doing up and down short flights for the past eight hours in the Caribbean, the tired number one flight attendant made the final welcome PA for the day.

"Ladies and gentlemen, on behalf of Allegiance Airlines, welcome to San . . . something."

✈

Here are some of the more noteworthy PA's we've heard lately:

A flight attendant who had had a very long day thought she was landing in Chicago—it was all blending together. At the last moment she remembered that she had arrived in Newark. Her announcement sounded like this: "Ladies and gentlemen, welcome to shit-Newark."

The following boarding announcement was made by a new Transglobal gate agent who was trying to let passengers know that Transglobal boarded its airplanes from aft to forward. "Ladies and gentlemen, we'll start with rows 22 through 30 because Transglobal enters from the rear."

It was the end of a long day, and this last leg of the trip promised to be a very busy one. There wasn't one vacant seat in forty rows of our DC10. To all of us, it seemed that we had to serve five thousand more people. This announcement was made immediately after take-off (for our benefit, and we laughed). "Ladies and gentlemen, the captain has turned off the No Smoking sign. Just as a reminder, rows 4 and 5 in first class, rows 10 and 11 in business class, and rows 34 to 120 in the main cabin are the designated smoking sections . . ."

Then there was the early-morning drunk demo given by a real party animal. Among other jewels was this: "If you want to adjust your seatbelt . . . go ahead and adjust it!"

Gone with
the Wind

The young woman had been
extremely demanding of us the entire flight.
Much more interested in the attractive male passenger
across the aisle than she was in caring for her infant daughter, she had repeatedly ordered us to take responsibility for
the baby.

"Flight attendant! Here, change my baby," she commanded as she thrust the baby into Dorothy's arms.

"Are you sure?" Dorothy was planning something, but
we didn't know what.

"Yes, I'm sure. CHANGE MY BABY! Just do it! OKAY?" the

woman answered, her loud voice becoming increasingly agitated.

"Okay." Dorothy walked to the rear of the airplane, handed us the baby, "borrowed" a black one from its parents, walked back to the woman, and said, "How's this?"

She changed her back before landing.

✈

All United States commercial flights bound for London arrive at either Heathrow Airport, just a few miles west of the city, or at Gatwick Airport, forty miles south. Gamma flight #22 had departed Atlanta and was bound for Gatwick.

The Gamma captain had been a twenty-year veteran with a flawless work record, but, through some unfortunate flight plan miscalculation, he found himself and the L1011 on final approach into Northrup Airport, about eighty miles north of where he should have been. Being four months away from retirement and his pot-of-gold pension, he was understandably dismayed at the possibility of termination for this serious faux pas.

"Sir, WHAT are your intentions?" the approach controllers at Northrup radioed as the unauthorized commercial carrier came in for a landing.

"Well," the captain began in a very southern drawl, "I think I'll jest open myself up a chicken farm."

✈

A flight attendant was running to the galley after the meal service with trays nearly stacked to the ceiling. A man who had made a pain of himself the entire flight pulled on her skirt and shouted, "Take this tray!"

She had had enough of him, so she did take his tray . . . but left the other nine on his tray table.

A passenger started screaming, and Barbara ran to find what the problem was.

"Oh, my God, look. There's a fly in my coffee. Do something about it!"

Barbara picked up the coffee cup to get a better look at it, then smiled at the woman and said jokingly, "No, no, ma'am, you're wrong. This is not a fly; this is part of our inflight entertainment. She's an Esther Williams impersonator. If you look closely, you'll see her doing the backstroke all around your cup."

That smartass was awarded a seven-day suspension.

A westbound Soaring Lion's 747 freighter overshot Los Angeles International Airport because the entire cockpit crew was asleep. By the time air traffic control was able to rouse them, they were forty minutes out over the Pacific.

All airline crews are extremely deferential to their captains. (Okay, so they're supposed to be.) No one ever wants to be brought up on an insubordination charge, so handling sensitive matters with kid gloves is basically the order of the day.

A Divided Airlines' 747 trip from Los Angeles to Tokyo was staffed with a crew of fourteen cabin attendants, six of whom were male. They had the pleasure of flying this particular trip with a captain known to be a real pain in the neck. He was forever needing more food and coffee refills.

The cabin crew were trying to complete their meal service and were justifiably annoyed when the captain interrupted them for the fifth time. A male flight attendant on board picked up the interphone in response to yet another crew call, and the captain began again.

"Could you bring some coffee up here?"

Having had enough, the flight attendant said, "Captain, do you know who this is?"

"Why, no," the captain answered, perplexed by the question.

Satisfied that his incognito status was secure, the flight attendant shouted, "Well, then, FUCK OFF!!"

✈

Will was loved by his fellow flight attendants for his personality, but when it came to work, he left a lot to be desired. In addition to being lazy, he had a tendency to be short and curt with the passengers.

Martin had had enough of him and decided to fix him once and for all. He handed Will a cup of coffee and said, "It might help you to move a bit faster." Of course, Will didn't know that Martin had placed two tablets of No-Doz in it.

Will could have done the entire service on this 747 by himself. He worked the front of the plane *and* both sides, and he wiped the galleys until the stainless steel counters were spotless. Unfortunately, the work-burst was a one-shot deal, but we love him anyway.

✈

A flight attendant had contracted crabs on a layover. He was in absolute agony and no relief was in sight until he got home. The four and a half hour flight seemed like an eternity.

At any given moment, he would disappear into the lavatory and scratch away. Panic was setting in with the thought of having to stay in the aisles and serve 200 more people. But by the third row, he had a system. As he prepared the drinks, he would position himself near the cart so he could rest his "problem area" against a seatback and sway to make the itching stop.

By mid-cabin, he got a bit sloppy and, instead of swaying from side-to-side on a seatback, he found himself stradling a bald-headed man who was now staring into his crotch.

He didn't dare try to explain the hazards of the new job to this man; he just left and locked himself into the lavatory until landing.

It was midwinter in Chicago; we had waited on the outer ramp in a blowing snowstorm for two hours for our gate and had just been radioed to expect at least another two-hour delay before we could move our inbound flight to the jetbridge.

The flight crew had had a long day, and we couldn't wait to get to our hotel rooms. Katie went to the cockpit to ask if she could bring the crew a beverage.

"Yes, three coffees, please. And maybe some Courvoisier, too," they ordered, chuckling the cockpit chuckle.

As a joke, Katie came back with three coffees—all with about an inch of liqueur in them. She stood there waiting for their surprised acknowledgement as one-by-one they took a sip.

With each thinking he must be the only one she gave the treat to, and not wanting to give up his blessed relief, not one said a word. They all just sipped and smiled.

Human nature is unpredictable.

Our appetizer for first class that day was shrimp cocktail. As this course is served first, before the tray is placed, a passenger was able to get up and come to us for more shrimp. He explained that he was extremely hungry and that the shrimp was delicious.

"I'm sorry, sir. We're all out," said a flight attendant turning to him with the tail of a shrimp hanging out of her mouth.

When we think about flight attendants who definitely live a jet-set life, Francine's name always comes up—lunch in the Caribbean, dinners in London, shopping in Paris. The girl has it all, including a great sense of humor.

Her recent beau, Jim, was a very big advertising mogul who kept insisting that she give up her career. He promised he would make it worthwhile. He needed a woman like her to entertain clients all over the world, which, he claimed, she couldn't do while working on an erratic schedule.

Jim had a very important party in San Francisco and insisted that Francine be there. As fate would have it, Francine was called to fly, but managed to get a layover in San Francisco. She could run to her hotel, shower, change, and just about make it.

Even experienced flight attendants don't always allow for Mother Nature's whims. On this particular night, Francine's flight was delayed two hours, giving her barely enough time to make the cocktail party. But she pulled it off. As soon as she landed in San Francisco, she disappeared into the plane's lavatory and, in true flight-attendant fashion, came out looking like a *Vogue* cover.

The next evening, before the flight home, Francine met the other flight attendants in a state of panic. "Did anyone pick up my uniform skirt last night? I was in such a rush, I must have left it in the lavatory." Francine laughed hard when they said no.

"Oh, boy, the passengers are in for a treat tonight. I guess I can kiss that skirt good-bye, anyway. The only ID I had on the inside label was 'TART-JFK,' instead of my name."

The labeling may have been more accurate that night than she anticipated. The only attire that she had to wear on the plane was a pair of skintight black leather pants to go with her uniform blouse.

Needless to say, the business cards were flying her way!

Final Approach

It was the captain's last flight of his thirty-four–year career with the airline. We'd given him a festive farewell party during the trip and made several PA announcements congratulating him on his nearing retirement.

His final approach had been a beautiful one, lovingly executed by a professional whose years of experience now culminated in one last touchdown. A split second before the DC10 would have made smooth contact with the tarmac, a powerful gust of wind sent the whole sequence out of kilter, slamming the plane onto the runway as if someone had tugged the rug out from under it. Applying full throttle, the captain pulled the plane's nose up, and we felt the main landing gear once again leave the runway.

Before we could speculate as to the near emergency this touch-and-go maneuver must have averted, the captain warmly said over the PA: "Ladies and gentlemen, just one more time—I want to get it right!!"

The "go-around" was completed; and to the cheers and applause of all of us, the DC10 settled softly onto the runway.

Because the cockpit door always stays locked during flight, part of every flight attendant's regulation equipment is a little cockpit key. It comes in handy when you have to enter the cockpit to serve food, pour coffee, introduce hijackers—those sorts of things.

The Air Orange Juice captain of a two-man Boeing 737 exited the cockpit to stretch his legs and use the lavatory. He had been gone for a few minutes when the first officer was radioed a weather update from one of the ground stations. It seems that they were going to be in for quite a bit of chop, since they would soon be flying through a massive cold front.

Knowing that turbulence severity is unpredictable, the co-pilot decided it would be prudent for both pilots to be at the controls. Having punched the crew call button several times to no avail, he stepped outside the cockpit to retrieve the captain and heard the cockpit door close with a click behind him.

As the two headed back to their little office in the front of the airplane, they made a quick joke about how two cockpit crew members minus two cockpit crew members equals zero cockpit crew members in the cockpit. Even funnier (ha! ha! ha!) was the fact (ha! ha! ha!) that they had both left their cockpit keys (ha! ha! ha!) in their uniform jackets, which were hanging in the (ha! ha! ha!) cockpit.

But not to worry. The flight attendants had theirs, did they not? The frantic search for the keys completed, the stony-faced flight attendants stood lined up in front of the captain shaking their heads no like the three little pigs.

Ha. Ha. Ha. They ended up breaking down the cockpit door with a fire axe. We're sure the happy campers looked forward to explaining the mess to management.

Connie was working the senior flight-attendant position on a DC10. Most of the first-class passengers had boarded when the captain and the first officer approached her in the middle of the cabin.

The captain was wearing sunglasses, carrying a blind "assist" stick, and being guided by one of the other flight-deck members. He was led up to Connie in front of all the first-class passengers and said, "Hi, Connie. My name is Mike, and I'm your captain today." Then, turning to his first officer, said, "Don, are we carrying cargo or passengers today?"

"Passengers, sir."

There were hysterical giggles as they fumbled their way to the cockpit. Apparently, though, not everyone was so delighted. Some spoilsport complained to the company, and they received three-day suspensions for that little performance.

The LaGuardia-based airplane mechanic was having a bad day. He had been working too many double shifts. As he drove his tug full speed ahead through the quarter-open hangar doors, he realized he had forgotten one small thing: to disengage the 727 he was dragging.

The resulting mess looked like a scene from *Airport*.

When visibility is low, commercial pilots are required to give periodic altitude updates to the tower during approach—"AA sixty-eight at twelve hundred," and so on.

Controllers are not known for their jolly humor on the job, unlike some pilots we know. On final approach to LaGuardia recently, this little exchange took place:

"Uh, Allegiance three-nine-four. Say altitude please."

Pause.

"Allegiance three-nine-four. Say altitude!"

"Al-ti-tude!"

"Allegiance three-nine-four, can you say vi-o-la-tion?"

Won't you be my neighbor?

The Federal Aviation Administration prescribes safe landing ceiling minimums for each airport in the country. When the cloud cover descends below these minimums, commercial landings are prohibited.

The ceiling at Denver's Stapleton Airport was varying so rapidly one day that we had already aborted landing twice. On our third and final try to set the plane down, the determined but crazed pilot announced to the already nervous passengers, "Okay folks, be sure your seatbelts are fastened tightly. We're gonna make a lunge for it!"

And wouldn't that inspire confidence?

✈

It was Sue Ann's first trip, and she had been assigned to the "midnight rocket" to Puerto Rico. Once all passengers were settled in their seats, one of the other flight attendants instructed her to pass out pillows and blankets.

"How do you say *pillow* and *blanket* in Spanish?" Sue Ann asked, wishing to communicate with the passengers in their own language. With a devious smile, the experienced flight attendant said, "Blanket is *manta* and pillow is *puta*."

As Sue Ann passed through with the pint-sized marshmallow puffs the airlines call pillows, softly saying from row to row "puta, puta," she couldn't understand why every man broke into hysterics and every woman looked horrified. John, one of her fellow workers, who was in earshot of her, quickly ushered her out of the aisles.

"Sue Ann, if I were you I wouldn't say that. That's the fastest way to be fired."

Petrified, she said, "What do you mean? That's what I was told to do—pass out all the pillows."

"Yes, honey, but not to advertise you're a whore. *Puta* means 'slut' in Spanish."

Needless to say, she got numerous propositions on that flight. What an indoctrination to flying!

✈

A new flight engineer obviously had not read his manual section on how to deal successfully with flight attendants. His overly frequent service requests and constant preaching on the offensiveness of gay stewards didn't exactly endear him to us. Rex, our head flight attendant that month, decided it was time to teach him a lesson.

The engineer called commanding that we bring up the cockpit meals. He told Rex that the captain wanted the chicken and that he would have the beef. Rex said, "Right away, sir," picked up the steak, dropped it on the floor, flipped it over, kicked it around, put it on the plate, then took it to the engineer.

"Here you are, sir. This is our Continental Filet. You'll find it has a tasty flavor like no other steak you've ever had in your life!"

We were amazed to see the engineer healthy enough to work the following trip.

✈

We were working a flight back from the Caribbean, and our inflight entertainment began—a PG movie to be enjoyed by all. We have a tendency to tune out what goes on in the movie, but that was impossible when a passenger grabbed a flight attendant and raved, "How COULD an airline show such a film?"

The attendant took in a few frames of the movie, then ran to turn it off. The ground personnel had played a joke on us, but good. Though she had expected to see a Walt Disney production, plastered before her eyes was *Deep Throat Revisited*.

Debbie may do Dallas, but we now know Isabella does the islands . . .

✈

A late passenger was trying to board the aircraft with an oversized garment bag. (We call them mobile homes or Winnebagos.) The flight attendant was explaining that there just was not enough room to accommodate it. The passenger started screaming, "Fuck you! I'm bringing this on the plane."

Never raising her voice, the flight attendant replied, "Sir, I don't care if you want to fuck me or not, but that bag is not coming on board this airplane."

Janet was flying the lower galley position (chief cook and bottle washer) on a DC10 coming into New York on New Year's Eve. She had what at the time seemed to be a pretty hot date.

After completing her service duties, she had about forty minutes to freshen up for her date, who was to pick her up at the airport. She told the head flight attendant, a big, funny guy named Billingsly, not to let anyone come downstairs via the little elevator because she would need some privacy.

She took off her uniform and all her makeup, rolled her hair in those pink, squashy curlers, brushed her teeth, and took a sponge bath in the galley sink.

There she was in all her glory as Billingsly himself came down—with a camera. She had to be nice to him from that day on . . . he threatened to post the picture in the crew lounge. Management prefers their flight attendants to remain clothed in flight. Something about assisting with possible emergencies . . .

Bye, Bye
Birdie

The New York/Miami run, the Kosher Klipper, is the most physically and mentally taxing trip in the system, and one particular passenger was so demanding that if the flight attendants could have opened the door midair, she would have been gone. It was never-ending: "Can I have a deck of cards? Where's my special meal? Do you have plastic wings?" On top of everything else, the weather was horrible going into Miami. People were getting violently ill everywhere. Finally, we touched down.

Ginny stood at the entry door for deplaning, and numerous passengers handed her used barf bags before leaving the aircraft. When the obnoxious woman came to the door and looked at the little white bags, she complained, "I didn't get one! How come I didn't get one of those?"

Grinning from ear to ear, Ginny handed her a full one and said, "A token of our appreciation for flying with us. Enjoy!"

✈

Whatever happened to the days when people used to get dressed up to travel? When flying used to be something special? The entire crew was amazed when a woman got on the plane with pink foam rollers and a hair net. To boot, she was a very demanding passenger.

The flight attendants were in the middle of the cocktail service, and her call button kept ringing through the cabin. Ted, annoyed with the incessant sound, went to find the source, hoping there wasn't a real problem. Noticing the disgusted look on her face, he approached the woman with the curlers and was greeted with, "Well, where's my drink?"

Not letting her get any further, he stuck his hand under the hair net and said, "No, no, no. Five more minutes under the dryer and you'll be done!" And he walked away . . .

✈

A teenage girl was sitting on the armrest of her seat with her butt protruding into the aisle. Every time the flight attendant passed by, he would ask her politely to move herself in. Eventually realizing that she did not understand a word of English, the next time he passed by he patted her butt and said smiling, "Ma'am, will you move your fat ass?"

This went on for about an hour, and finally he smacked

her on the butt and, once again with a smile, bent down and whispered in her ear, "Will you move your fucking fat ass!"

She smiled and repositioned herself in her seat. It was like a scene from National Lampoon's *European Vacation*.

✈

Jerry, a male flight attendant who left no doubt as to his sexual orientation, had obviously lost his mind one day when he put on a female flight attendant's navy pumps. Carrying a fruit salad special meal on his head, he pranced down the aisle in search of the meal's owner.

Carmen Miranda, step aside!

✈

The Boston/Washington, D.C. flight was always full of senators and business executives laden with huge piles of magazines and newspapers. A smartass flight attendant approached a senator from Massachusetts. "Senator, do you honestly think you'll do all of that reading during a fifty-five minute flight?"

"Why, yes. I took Evelyn Wood's Speed Reading Course."

Something must have snapped. The flight attendant answered, "Well, those courses aren't worth much. I took the Mark Eden Bust Development Course and look what it's done for me!" She opened her jacket and flashed her still minimal equipment at him.

✈

During a lengthy delay at the gate in Chicago, everyone was restless. We heard the captain make this announcement over the PA: "Ladies and gentlemen, the machine we normally use to pummel and mutilate your luggage is temporarily broken, so we're having to do it by hand. We should be leaving shortly . . . looks like there's not much left."

We loved it!

The fun-loving crew had been discussing the fact that no one ever watched the safety demo.

During the next demo, Katherine had a hard time finishing the PA because the flight attendant in first class did the oxygen decompression part using one of those plastic pig nose things attached to an elastic headband. She thought she'd die when he put the thing over his nose and mouth and told passengers to breathe normally.

And not a soul in the cabin noticed!

We love the Leastearn Airlines' captain who had had enough of the air traffic control delay bullshit. He just taxied his aircraft back to the gate, declared, "I quit," and got off.

Now that's going out in style.

Epilogue

Ladies and gentlemen, in just a few minutes we will be landing. At this time we would like to take a moment to say a few words.

We can only hope that the next time a ticket agent ignores you, your departure gate changes at the last minute, you're sitting on the runway for three hours, or someone has parked himself in your assigned seat, you can remember a story or two and chuckle to yourself.

To make light of the chaotic world of commercial aviation was our intent. We both realize what each of you goes through, since we have been with the airlines for eighteen years. Together, we all have endured deregulation. *We do understand.*

A canceled flight on Christmas Eve means we'll see yet another hotel room instead of being at home with our friends and families, a two-hour delay doesn't quite set the mood for a "calm trip" for us, and if we had our way, half the plane *would* be set aside to accommodate your luggage.

Of course, there are many different personalities in our flight crew ranks, but the bad apples are few and far between. Most of us care a lot; that's why we're here. No matter what we may jokingly say to each other, you can bet that when the chips are down, we'll be there for *you.*

We hope you've enjoyed sharing a bit of our world. May all your flights leave on time, and remember: The chicken dish is usually your best bet!

Happy flying!!

If you've an inflight experience you'd like to share with us, send it to:

CABIN PRESSURE
c/o Thomas Dunne Books
175 Fifth Avenue
New York, NY 10010

READ
MY
LIPS.

The Wit & Wisdom of
GEORGE
BUSH

With some reflections by Dan Quayle

edited by Ken Brady & Jeremy Solomon

THE WIT & WISDOM OF GEORGE BUSH
Brady & Solomon, eds.
  91687-6 $2.95 U.S. _____ 91688-4 $3.95 Can.

Publishers Book and Audio Mailing Service
P.O. Box 120159, Staten Island, NY 10312-0004

Please send me the book(s) I have checked above. I am enclosing
$ _____ (please add $1.25 for the first book, and $.25 for
each additional book to cover postage and handling. Send check
or money order only—no CODs.)

Name_____

Address_____

City_____ State/Zip_____

Please allow six weeks for delivery. Prices subject to change
without notice.

BUSH 9/89

MAMA WARNED YOU
ABOUT GIRLS LIKE THIS

Meet screenwriter Anna Kate O'Shea. Rich and pretty, wild and witty, right now she's "between pictures," basking in the glow (and the cash) from her last hit film. From the Academy Awards to Cannes, from New York to California, this not-so-simple girl from Texas embraces the lifestyles of the rich and shameless, looking for love in all the wrong places. She's even thinking of calling her next film *The Boyfriend Who Came From Hell*. It's fun when life's a perpetual party, but the guests have been getting a little ridiculous....

Between PICTURES
Jayne Loader

"A literary Madonna, Jayne Loader is knockdown funny and smart. Hot, sexy, and a fabulous new voice in fiction."
> —Rhoda Lerman,
> author of *The Book of the Night* and *Ellen: A Novel*

LANDMARK BESTSELLERS
FROM ST. MARTIN'S PAPERBACKS

HOT FLASHES
Barbara Raskin
_____ 91051-7 $4.95 U.S.   _____ 91052-5 $5.95 Can.

MAN OF THE HOUSE
"Tip" O'Neill with William Novak
_____ 91191-2 $4.95 U.S.   _____ 91192-0 $5.95 Can.

FOR THE RECORD
Donald T. Regan
_____ 91518-7 $4.95 U.S.   _____ 91519-5 $5.95 Can.

THE RED WHITE AND BLUE
John Gregory Dunne
_____ 90965-9 $4.95 U.S.   _____ 90966-7 $5.95 Can.

LINDA GOODMAN'S STAR SIGNS
Linda Goodman
_____ 91263-3 $4.95 U.S.   _____ 91264-1 $5.95 Can.

ROCKETS' RED GLARE
Greg Dinallo
_____ 91288-9 $4.50 U.S.   _____ 91289-7 $5.50 Can.

THE FITZGERALDS AND THE KENNEDYS
Doris Kearns Goodwin
_____ 90933-0 $5.95 U.S.   _____ 90934-9 $6.95 Can.

Publishers Book and Audio Mailing Service
P.O. Box 120159, Staten Island, NY 10312-0004

Please send me the book(s) I have checked above. I am enclosing
$ _____ (please add $1.25 for the first book, and .25 for each
additional book to cover postage and handling. Send check or
money order only—no CODs.)

Name _____

Address _____

City _____ State/Zip _____

Please allow six weeks for delivery. Prices subject to change
without notice.

BEST 1/89